A DANGEROUS JOB

A SCREAM RINGS OUT close by. I feel a rush of air by my face and a thud on my foot. When I look down, Jimmy has crumpled atop my leg. His eyes are closed, and his mouth twists to one side as if the screams have fled, leaving him empty.

When I look down at the hand he cradles, something is missing. White bone glares like a naked truth, like a streak of pure lightning in a dark sky.

A spasm shakes my chest. I swallow hard to force my dinner back down before I scream as loud as I can. "Mr. Godbold! Mr. Godbold, come quick! The spinner has taken his thumb!"

January
1905

KATHARINE BOLING

January
1905

HARCOURT, INC.

Orlando   Austin   New York   San Diego   Toronto   London www.HarcourtBooks.com

First Harcourt paperback edition 2005

Grateful acknowledgment is made to the Prints and
Photographs Division, National Child Labor Committee
Collection, of the Library of Congress for the use of two
photographs by Lewis W. Hine: page opposite the title
page, LC-USZ62-49601; page opposite the afterword,
LC-USZ62-96800.

The Library of Congress has cataloged the hardcover
edition as follows:
Boling, Katharine.
January 1905/Katharine Boling.
p. cm.
Summary: In a 1905 mill town, eleven-year-old twin sisters,
Pauline, who goes to work with the rest of the family, and
Arlene, whose crippled foot keeps her home doing the
cooking, cleaning, and washing, are convinced that the other
sister has an easier life until a series of incidents helps them
see each other in a new light.
[1. Child labor—Fiction.   2. Sisters—Fiction.
3. Twins—Fiction.   4. Family life—Fiction.]   I. Title.
PZ7.B6359117Jan   2004
[Fic]—dc22   2003024470
ISBN-13: 978-0-15-205119-8 ISBN-10: 0-15-205119-8
ISBN-13: 978-0-15-205121-1 pb ISBN-10: 0-15-205121-X pb
H G F E D C B A

Printed in the United States of America

January
1905

ONE

I AM FULL OF HATE, and that, I know, is wicked. When my mother wakens me, it already bubbles in my throat like a spring ready to overflow.

"Get up, Pauline. It's time."

My feet strike the cold floor as I tumble out of bed. Glancing back in the dark, I see my sister still under the warm quilt, her hands curled on the pillow like sleeping birds.

The mill whistle begins like a woman sobbing before changing to a long wail. It prods me into dressing. As I raise my nightdress over my head, the chill seizes me, so I hurry to pull on my undershirt, drawers, and then my dress. I put everything out the night before, so the cold has less time to grab me.

I leave off my shoes. I have learned to bargain with myself. If I take the time to put them on, I miss first chance at the privy and have to stand waiting, my whole self growing icier still.

Mama has started the stove, the fire glowing red, and the warmth calls to me, but the other call is louder, and I step out onto the frozen ground past the cabbage rows glistening with frost.

The outhouse door creaks like I woke it and it does not want to be bothered. *Stop your complaining. It is I, not you, who must find the seat in the dark and start the pee from my shaking body down the black hole.*

———

ON THE STEPS outside, my brother waits, his frosty breath drifting. I feel a rush of air as he brushes by. Josh has not learned my trick about the shoes, so he is second.

The moon still hangs, a sliver, like someone slit the sky, and stars spill out like bright stuffing.

Since it is warm in the stove room, I guess it is no matter that I have to wait by the sink while Daddy washes his face. My stomach churns at the smell of the bacon, but all in good time.

I curl my toes as I bide my time behind Daddy. Some feeling comes back to them as I watch him scoop big dripping handfuls from the pail. He is missing two fingers on his right hand. Mama frowns at him because water sloshes onto the floor and puddles under the sink. She leaves the bacon frying on the stove to hand him a towel.

The kerosene lamp shines on her face. I do not know what time Mama gets up, only that she is already dressed and the fire made when she calls me in the mornings. If I did not know better, I would think she sleeps in her clothes.

By the time Josh and I have washed up, Mama has put the plates of grits, each with a curl of bacon, on the table. She hands around biscuits left over from supper, and if I push mine into the grits, it takes on some of the heat, like it was fresh made.

We bow our heads. Daddy says, "Thank you, Lord, for breakfast. Amen."

Josh and Daddy make snuffling noises as they eat. Josh has no patience with a fork for grits. He ladles his in with a tablespoon. Mama looks down at her plate. She takes in a long breath before she starts to eat.

My tongue burns with my haste, and my

stomach fills with heat. We are busy with our breakfast, making our mouths too full for talk. I have barely swallowed the last of it before we rise from the table.

Mama calls into our room, "Good-bye, Arlene. We're going now."

I say nothing. How would she hear? She is still sleeping. *Yes, we're leaving now. The dark still hunkers over the mill, but we're going out into the blackness while you, the favored one, sleep as late as you like. Enjoy the warmth of the quilt and the soft bed, while the shape of me there grows cold.*

I have never counted the steps to the mill. I know only that the number of steps is different every morning. Today the cold bites through my sweater and swirls around my legs as I try to keep up with Mama. Josh and Daddy push way ahead of us with their long steps.

Margaret and Katie pass in the dark.

They're best friends, eleven like me, and Katie has her younger brother Jimmy by the hand. He stumbles along half asleep. I do not think they see me.

Sometimes I wish there were only one of them—Katie or Margaret. With one of them, I might be her best friend, but as it is, that place is already taken.

For the walk to the mill, I have left my hate behind in the warm bed with my sister. I will call for it when I need it. Arlene will wake to find the room warm and her breakfast on the back of the stove. She only has to make the beds and wash the dishes before she starts to cook.

By the time she comes to bring our dinner pails at noon, the sun will have made a watery path to the top of the sky, and I will have tied more threads than I can count.

I AM FULL OF HATE, and that, I know, is wicked. When my mother wakes Pauline, it already bubbles in my throat, ready to overflow.

"Get up, Pauline. It's time."

The whistle blows like a giant owl hooting before he goes to bed. *To-whoo, to-whoo,* trailing off as he flies through the woods.

I cannot fly. Pauline cannot fly. In that, we are the same. Like our mouths and eyes, like the jut of our chins. Like the part in our hair. Everything about us is the same. Only not.

They think I am sleeping, but I peer out under my lashes at Pauline as she throws off her nightdress and puts on her clothes. Her body makes a blur in the dim room, but I know from memory how straight she is down to the soles of her feet. I know how she can hop and jump like a rabbit or scurry like a startled mouse.

They may think I'm asleep, but I have to stay awake to keep from wetting the bed. My turn comes later, after the rest have gone.

But now bumping noises sound throughout the house, and I know what each one means. I hear Daddy's heavy shoes *clunk* and Josh's quicker *thud*s, and the pots in the stove room *clink.* The sounds connect me to their morning.

The house grows quiet again. I can imagine everyone around the kitchen table in the lamplight, can smell the salty bacon. Only the click of a spoon on a bowl punctures the quiet. At least I'm out of the way.

I hear the chairs scrape and a shuffling of shoes.

Mama comes to the bedroom door. "Good-bye, Arlene. We're going now."

Pauline says nothing. She is glad to be gone, gone to be with Katie and Margaret, who also work at the mill. She will laugh with them and talk all the way there while I am left to myself for the day.

The front door slams. *Good-bye, Arlene. Good-bye, Arlene. We're going now. We're going now.* The words echo in my head. I throw back the quilt. Still in my nightclothes I hobble through the warm stove room, with its jumble of dirty plates and pots, and out the back door.

I try to hurry, but the monster foot drags at me, holding me back. In the street, people rush to the mill. I wonder if they see me, register me, see me struggling with that foot, know where I am going in the cold, or wonder why I did not have the sense to put my clothes on first. The cold rushes under my nightdress, but I cannot afford to feel it. I must hurry, hurry.

Finally I open the creaking door and sit, relieved that only a little pee has dribbled down my leg.

Even though I am alone now, I dress before breakfast, take my time, pulling up the quilt and spreading the bed. I fix the pillows straight, hers and mine. I pull on the shoes. On my right foot, a shoe like Pauline wears. On the left, one Josh has outgrown, because the monster foot has its own shape that will not be forced into a smaller shoe.

Before we were born, when did it happen? When did it become my foot and not hers? Did she wrest a good one from me in exchange for the one I have? I should like to ask her if she remembers. Or was it when my mother named us? This is Pauline the perfect one, and this one we will call Arlene because of her monster foot.

The grits are stiff; the bacon, warm and limp. I eat the grits straight out of the tin pot from the back of the stove, a biscuit tucked to one side. A little coffee remains, strong, bitter, and full of grounds, but I drink it out of Daddy's cup before I begin to wash up.

TWO

B<small>Y THE TIME MAMA</small> and I get to the spinning room, the cold has left me unfeeling, and the heat of the mill is welcoming. At first the warmth wraps me like the stove room at home, but soon the noise of the machines creeps into my very bones, making them shake like chattering teeth.

I will take off my sweater, but not yet. I will wait for the cold to go away. Not yet, but the turning bobbins way above my head call to me, the whole giant wall of them screams, *Look at me! Look at me!*

Not yet. I wait for the whistle.

I'll look at you long enough. I'll look at you twelve hours today. That is enough.

The bobbins spin, gathering their thread, pulling it, growing fat without me. The whistle blows again. It is time to look. I cannot ignore them any longer.

We begin our watching, waiting, walking, prying, for when the thread breaks, we must clamber up top to find the parted ends and tie them back so the bobbins can go on spinning, reeling, filling up.

The lint piles up around the bobbins, and we have to dust it away. It gathers on the floor and slides beneath our shoes. It swirls in the air like a swarm of gnats, up my nose and on my dress, and I cannot rid myself of it. The sweepers push the lint into piles, their brooms taller than they are.

Edwin is the youngest of the sweepers. Sometimes I think he forgets what he is doing. When he has cornered the lint, he walks away, his broom trailing, and he stands by the window, his arm wrapped around the broom handle, his thumb in his mouth.

If the supervisor, Mr. Godbold, catches him sucking his thumb and staring outside like that, the old man flies at him in a rage, cuffing the boy about the head before leading him back by the ear to the pile of fluff on the floor.

Mr. Godbold has one lazy eye, and I cannot always tell when he is looking at me. He combs his hair into a rolling pompadour in front, thick like his bushy eyebrows. His good eye he fixes on us as he walks between the machines. He shouts at us over the noise. "Jimmy, there! Look sharp!"

One of the doffer boys, his trousers rolled, climbs with bare feet and snaps an empty bobbin into the place of the fat one he hauls down.

"Pauline, there! Quick!"

I stretch to catch the two pieces of broken thread and tie them together so that the whirling can continue.

I do not like Mr. Godbold. He touched me once as I climbed to the spools. He touched me in a way I knew he should not, and when I turned around, I did not try to find his good eye, for I saw him grin, and I shuddered, saying nothing. It does not do to make trouble. I just stay out of his way and try to do what he says. *Pauline, there! Quick!* I'm always quick when he calls.

Mr. Godbold may think he tells us what to do, but the thread is in charge here. It yanks us around as surely as if we were tied to it. I check one side and walk the other. I work only one row of machines, though Mama has three on the far end of the room. She can reach what I have to climb for, my hands careful of the spinning spools.

Because the thread is master, the heat in the room warms it, not us. The windows are shut tight, for the cold would make the thread brittle. Soon the spinning room grows as hot as our stove room on bath night, when steam rises in our faces and makes it hard to breathe. I take off my sweater and wish I could take off more.

Windows fill the spinning room wall, but for what? We cannot open them or see through them. The sky through the lint and grime is like a fuzzy picture.

At home Arlene can see the sky clear.

I think of Arlene, and my hate flies straight to me, finds me again. She has only the washing and cooking. *All because of her foot. But for mine I'd be home, too, where I could sit when I wanted to, have a drink of water, go out to the privy. But no. Because I have two good feet, I must walk and watch from six until noon, from one until six, careful of the younger boy sweeping.*

THE CHICKENS LOOK at me with suspicion as I scrape the grits pot clean onto the ground before them. One pecks at the shoe on my good foot before she ambles over to the white congealed mess. *It isn't fine kernel corn, but, after all, you didn't have to pay for it at the company store. You didn't have to cook it this morning in the dark, so be grateful. Eat! Hush your clucking.*

Four rooms make up our house, three bedrooms and the one we live in, the stove room. The lint would soon fill the house up, I think, if I did not stay watchful. I reach under our bed with the broom. Behind the slop jar. Behind Josh's other old shoe. *Come out. You can't hide under there!* No one invites the lint in. It rides unbidden from the mill on their clothes like beggar lice catch a ride from the field. Everyone shakes it off or combs it out, and it gathers in flocks under beds, on the top of Mama's dresser, and in corners, where it tries to conceal itself. As I come closer the fuzz lifts as if it would fly, but it settles again, agreeing to ride the broom straws.

Once the dishes are washed and put away, I have used all the water, so I take the pail out to the pump in front. The cold makes the pump sluggish, and the metal handle is ice under my palm. The sun has begun its slow climb, but I shiver as I clump back to the house with the pail. Water sloshes over the rim, and the handle bites into my hand.

While I wait for the water to heat, I go out back for more wood, filling my arms with the rough, prickly pieces. They smell of turpentine. I bang my right heel as I ease in the back door. Josh spent most of Saturday afternoon splitting wood, the ax ringing as it thudded, sending splinters flying. I stacked the splinters in a pile for later; they are good for starting fires.

I let the fire go out once, so supper was late and everyone grew cross. I am more careful now. The water steams in the sink. The dirty clothes bloom on the floor. Josh's shirt, the torn sleeve mended, goes in first.

Mama had said, "What a shame. A good shirt." She drew the stitches up tight.

Daddy frowned. "Better his shirt than his arm."

Mama drew her lips tight, too. "That is true. Far better."

"I'll get the scissors," I said.

"Never mind." Mama twisted the thread around her hand, popping the thread, leaving a fine white line around her fist.

The washboard thumps against the sink. I scrub, my nostrils filled with the odor of strong soap, my knuckles stinging where I miss the shirt and scrape the board. Overalls are hardest. So I put them off until last. *I will wrestle you. I will scrub you with no mercy. Then I will wring you dry and hang you on the line in the cold to repent. I will wrestle you, and I will win.*

My hands are still smarting from the soap and the cold when I start dinner.

Four dinner pails in a row on the table—Daddy's, Josh's, Mama's, and Pauline's. Today I'm cooking backbone and rice, with cabbage on the side. I would surprise them and bake a sponge cake, but the sugar is gone. Daddy said not to put anything else we didn't have to have on the books at the store. I know he would say we could do without sugar for another week at least.

THREE

Mr. GODBOLD WATCHES US closely as the time draws near to noon. He does not want one move toward the door before the whistle. He wants not one thread dangling when we stop for dinnertime. He wants not one fluff of lint under the bobbins, not one piece of lint on the floor.

Perspiration dampens the back of my neck, and my shoulders ache. I can feel my stomach rumble, and the bottoms of my feet smart from climbing. I do not need a clock. I know it is noon. *Where is the woman's cry? Ah, the whistle moans and wails, and I am free! Free of the heat and the stifling air, free of the noise that rings in my head. Free of Mr. Godbold!*

I look for Katie and Margaret. We fly down the stairs, blinking in the light. The cold finds my damp dress collar to remind me I left my sweater behind. Katie wrestles into her jacket sleeves, but I will not go back, will not enter the spinning room until the whistle screams again.

Mama and the other women eat their dinner in a room close by the spinning room, but we girls flee the building for a corner out of the wind where the sun shines. We squat there to wait for our dinner. Katie's younger brother staggers with the weight of the pail he hands her, and Margaret gets hers from her father. He is red-eyed and sour, and he has nothing to say as he hands hers to her.

Daddy calls Margaret's father a tin-bucket toter because he does not work. He sends Margaret, her mother, and four other girls off to the mill in the morning while he fishes or lounges at home. Arlene says he sometimes sits in the company store drinking beer and eating pigs' feet and crackers. She should know because she often goes there for the groceries. I am sure she lingers for the gossip, too.

But Margaret's daddy does bring dinner to them.

I peer around the corner looking for Arlene.

"I brought my ball and jackstones," Katie says to Margaret. "Want to play after dinner?"

Margaret nods, her dark braids bobbing.

Katie's jackstones are dull. The ball, the color of rust. I should like my own, but they are forty cents at the company store, and I have only the few cents Daddy can spare for me on payday. That is not enough for the shiny new ones and the bright red ball.

I would like to play, but they have not asked me. Perhaps if I had my own jackstones, they would want to play with the new ones with me.

At home Mama would make me say the blessing, but we do not want to waste time here. Katie opens her pail, and the smell of chicken and dumplings floats in the sheltered space. She takes out a square of yellow corn bread, and soon I hear her smacking. I try not to watch, angry I do not yet have my dinner.

Margaret opens her pail and screws up her face. "Not pinto beans again. My daddy's a terrible cook. And he's gone and burned the corn pone." She slumps. "He even left out the spoon."

Where is Arlene? Then I see her, the sun flashing on a pail, making it look like a light wobbling toward us. My stomach churns, and my mouth waters as Arlene comes closer.

The girls look up. Katie has yellow crumbs on her chin and the corner of her mouth. She covers her mouth and giggles. "Your sister walks like she's drunk."

Margaret snickers, bending over her beans and dark bread. "Like a frog, like a crippled frog." Her plaits swing as she moves her head in rhythm to Arlene's walk. *"Ker-hop, ker-flop. Ker-hop, ker-flop."* She shakes her head.

"Like a *drunk* crippled frog," Katie says.

As Arlene draws nearer, Margaret says under her breath, *"Ker-hop, ker-plop. Ker-hop, ker-plop."*

They giggle once more like they have no control. I laugh, too. I want to play jacks, so I join in, bending double with mirth.

When Arlene hands me my pail, I peer in. The biscuit on top plumps brown.

Underneath, the rice grains shine like pearls in the sun. I pull out the spoon and lick off the handle. I do not look at Arlene. I do not want her shame. She is too close. I might catch it from her.

Before I plunge my spoon into my rice, I speak to Arlene. I speak loud, so the others will hear and let me play. "You're late!"

I PUT AN EXTRA BISCUIT on top of Daddy's and Josh's pails. That way maybe they will not miss cake. I do not wait for the noon whistle to hoot but leave the house early.

The buckets swing as I limp my way to the mill, past the identical white houses. I think I am the first one on the road with the buckets, but I must hurry because I am slow. *But like the tortoise, I shall win.*

As soon as the whistle blows, some folks will stream from the mill, going home to get their dinner pails—for some of the houses are empty all day, with everyone at work. I suppose their dinners are cold, sorry things with nobody home to cook them. I look up at the windows of the spinning room. The sun glints on them, making them shine like beacons. *Inside is warm. Pauline is warm. Out of the wind that bites. Warm with Katie and Margaret, Mama, Josh, Daddy, and the others.*

The whistle hoots. The carding room is full of confusion as the men and boys rush past. I keep an eye out for Daddy and Josh.

Josh has just been sent up to carding. He puffs out his chest with importance. When he came home with the torn sleeve, he wore it like a medal. He had come that close to the rumbling pulleys, had dared them, like in a game—*Snake in the gutter, eating bread and butter.*

I could never play the snake. I am not quick enough. But Josh had always teased the snake in our games in the road after supper, and I bet he taunted the pulley the same way, jerking back his arm, hearing cloth rip. So close for a dare.

Daddy finds me first. He already has his daily quota of lint in his hair, on his shirt, clinging like snowflakes. And Josh, also, right behind Daddy. But I know about that kind of snow, too stubborn to melt, and I know I will see it at home soon enough.

Josh opens his pail to see the two biscuits, buttered hot. He grins at me, his hair a tousled mess. Daddy puts his hand on my shoulder as he takes his pail. Above the noise it is hard to hear him, but it feels like a thank-you to me.

Mama is easier to find. She and Miss Ethel are already sitting in their room off the spinning room, where the grown women gather for lunch. Miss Ethel's red hair is easy to spot.

Mama smiles, the corners of her eyes crinkling as she takes her pail.

"Hello, Arlene," Miss Ethel says. She plays the piano at church on Sundays.

No one ever calls me Pauline by mistake. The year we went to school, the teacher straight off got it right, but sometimes when we sat at our desks, I'd see her glance at the floor before she called my name.

Once at recess, Pauline got behind me. I could not see what she was doing, but the other children could, and I saw them laughing. Even the teacher smiled. I turned around to see Pauline imitating the way I walk, dragging her foot along. P *is for* perfect—*Pauline.* A *is for* awkward—*Arlene.*

I would like to stay with Mama, Miss Ellen, and the others, listen to them talk, but I know Pauline waits, know she is hungry and waiting.

There they sit, the three of them— Pauline, Margaret, and Katie. Katie's hair is so blond, when the light strikes it she looks like she wears a halo. They giggle like someone told a joke. I wish I had been close enough to hear a good joke. I have not laughed today. I have seen nothing all that funny, although Katie has corn bread crumbs on her chin, giving her a yellow goatee. I start to smile, but that is just my joke. I think they have another one.

FOUR

THEY INVITE ME to join the game after all. We have played three sets of jackstones. I won one set, but I let Katie and Margaret win the other two.

We were playing crack the eggs. I tossed the ball and picked up a jack, tapping it on the ground before I caught the ball. On purpose, I brushed my dress with my hand. They didn't seem to notice. "Didn't you see my clothes burn?" I asked.

Margaret's plaits whipped around her face as she shook her head.

"I did. I've fouled out." I handed over the jackstones.

The other time, I caught the ball in both my hands.

Katie squealed, "You missed. You're out!"

They do not want a friend who always beats them at their game. The whistle sounds. Katie chases down the ball, which has rolled away from us, and swoops up the rest of the jackstones to put into her pocket. I am full from dinner, but I am getting cold, and we scramble to our feet. Mr. Godbold will know if we are not in our places by the time the whistle stops.

Margaret and Katie dash to the other side of the spinning room, Katie shrugging off her jacket. I wish I worked at the far end. Then I could see the other girls when I rounded the corner. I could smile or make a face, but I have only Jimmy and Edwin, the sweeping boy, and Mr. Godbold at my end. Carrie is next to me, separated from Katie and Margaret by two other rows. She is older, and she has her mind on other things, but she manages three machines.

Jimmy clambers to the top like a monkey showing off, his bare dirty feet in my face. He grins.

The cold goes away, and the stifling heat returns. Five more hours of thread and bobbins and lint. I try not to think of Arlene going home to eat her dinner in peace. Or perhaps she eats it first, before she brings the pails. *Hot. Right off the stove, the rice steaming, the biscuits melting the butter before her eyes, the cabbage still crisp at the edges.* Yes, that is what she does, picking out the fat little pieces of meat, looking through the rice, rooting through the pot. That is why she seemed in no hurry to leave me and Katie and Margaret. She had filled her belly already.

And now she has gone home to sleep in

the afternoon. I bristle at the thought. A thread pops. The bobbins spin high.

"Pauline!"

I climb. Mr. Godbold slouches off.

To my right I see someone new, a stranger, lean faced and bright-eyed, his hair parted precisely in the middle. Dressed in a suit, he is free of lint. He carries a stand and a camera like those at the Fourth of July picnic. In a flash he disappears behind a black cloth, and he points at me. I freeze. He moves quickly and aims at Jimmy mounting for a full bobbin. Afterward he points at the sweeping boy.

Mr. Godbold reappears. Seeing the stranger, he puts his hands on his hips as if he cannot make sense of what's happening. He balls up his hands into fists, rushing at the man. The stranger moves faster, leaving as quick as he came. He must be used to angry supervisors.

Scowling, Mr. Godbold turns back. He yells at me and Jimmy. "What are you gawking at? Get back to work!"

The stranger has stolen my picture and carried it away with him. What will he do with it? Why does he want it? *Like my sister who shares my image to mock me. Will he change another part of me? Three sisters will exist then: One, Pauline who walks around inside of me. Another, Arlene, who is the adored one, allowed to do so little. And now this third. Perhaps she'll have a lazy eye like Mr. Godbold.*

I have five more hours to think about it.

I THINK OF PAULINE, her dinner brought to her to eat out in the sun. With Katie and Margaret, Pauline can tell jokes and not worry if the laundry is done or the pots washed.

The thought of my own dinner calls me. I hurry home. The pots in the sink yell to me. The overalls and dresses on the line say my name over and over. *Arlene! Arlene! Faster! Faster!*

But the voice calling to me is real. "Arlene! Arlene!"

The flood of folks that swelled at noon has

passed, and few walk in the street. Which one called my name? When I turn I see old Bertha Franklin beckoning, her crooked fingers waving me to her.

Miss Bertha, our granny woman, comes when someone is sick. The doctor knows little, Mama says. *Who needs Miss Bertha now?* When I was younger, I thought of her as a witch, but now I know she does only good, that she uses her witchcraft to outwit the sickness. Once when I had a fever, she sat by my bed and soothed my head with compresses and sweated the heat from me.

When I move in her direction, she hides one hand in the pocket of her ragged jacket, tightens her hold on the satchel she carries, and waits, patting her foot on the hard red clay of the road.

She calls to me in a raspy voice. "It's Frances. She sent word. I'll need help." Her face reminds me of a dried apple—still red but wrinkled, her eyes like two black shiny seeds. Her bottom lip pokes out with snuff. "It's her time."

What of the mess in the stove room at home? What of the washing? But I do what I think Mama would say, and I follow Miss Bertha to one of the mill houses half a block from ours. I have not seen Mrs. Harrell in several months, not at the company store or in the room behind the spinning one where Mama and the others eat their dinner, but we hear her as soon as we step onto the stoop. She bellows like a cow past milking time. It raises the hair on the back of my neck.

"We'll not bother knocking," Miss Bertha says over her shoulder as she opens the door. She turns to the left as we enter the hall.

Mrs. Harrell's house is just like ours

inside and out, and I feel at home. It even smells like ours—of stale cabbage and fatback. Only the beds are different.

In the room on the left, the bawling stops and Mrs. Harrell looks at us wild-eyed, her face screwed up, her hair in her eyes. Her neck and forehead glisten with perspiration, and she has thrown off the covers. The sheet and quilt hang crooked and onto the floor. I can see her swollen belly under her nightclothes.

"Build up the fire," Miss Bertha says to me. "Put water to boil on the stove. We're going to have a young'un before supper time."

Miss Bertha has already laid down her satchel and shed her jacket, folding it neatly on the back of a chair. She bends down, and opening her bag, she takes out a knife, its blade flashing in the weak light. My heart catches in my throat. What will she do? But she stoops farther, to slide the knife under the bed. "To cut the pain," she explains.

I go to the stove room to follow her directions, prying up the lid to add wood. The match smells of rotten eggs, and the fire does not want to catch. But I blow on it and little sparks take life from my breath to rise up, curl, and fall away. I blow again. This time more sparks, more red. It will catch. I take up a pail and head out the front, to the pump by the street.

When I come in, Miss Bertha has righted the covers of Mrs. Harrell's bed and sits in a straight chair beside it. Mrs. Harrell lies on her side, facing Miss Bertha. They talk.

Mrs. Harrell sweeps her hair aside. "I did not take Roy his dinner."

Miss Bertha sniffs. "He can do without his dinner pail one day." She takes a hairbrush from the dresser and pulls it through Mrs. Harrell's hair, braiding it into one long plait. "Where's Percy?"

"Asleep."

Miss Bertha puts her hand on Mrs. Harrell's belly as I go back out the door.

Each time I make a trip for another pail and pass by the bedroom, I feel like an intruder. They whisper together, Mrs. Harrell's words coming in quick gasps and then more bawling, like she will frighten the baby out. I am curious and afraid for her, but I have my job, and soon I have two great pots full of water on the stove, and I sink with relief into a chair. All the calling and loud crying makes me nervous, and I think to tidy the kitchen like Mama would. As soon as the water boils, I'll wash the breakfast dishes that still sit on the table amid a glob of congealed grits.

Miss Bertha comes in, looks at the stove, nodding with approval. She carries a sheet and hands it to me. "Here. Tear this into rags. We'll need them soon."

Though old and threadbare, the sheet does not tear easily, and I grip it, pulling with all my strength until the fabric gives way. The sound of the sheet ripping joins the crackle of the fire. Bubbles rise in the water. I stack the folded rags on a chair and get up to do the dishes.

FIVE

CARRIE WORKS THE THREE machines just down from me. She pins up her long dark hair. At sixteen she is sweet on George, who works with Daddy and Josh in the carding room. George rushes over at dinnertime with his pail, and he and Carrie sit outside, apart from us. Sometimes I see George hold out a spoonful to her or share a piece of pie. Carrie says they will get a four-room house someday and take in a boarder. That way they could afford to pay the rent the mill charges for the houses. They want to get married, but Carrie's mama and daddy say they are too young.

George is two years older than Josh, and I cannot imagine Josh with a wife. What time he has away from work, he uses to go up to the river, fishing, or to play taggy with the other boys. They drive a stake into the ground, set another on it whirling, and when the second stake spins up, they strike it with a bat to see how far it will go. They yell and call a lot and slap one another on the back.

No, I don't think Josh thinks of a wife, but what do I know of Josh? I don't know him that well. It's been mostly Arlene and me. *Are you sleeping now, lazy sister?*

"Catch it there!" Mr. Godbold calls. "Hurry! Pick up your feet!"

Now that the light slants low through the windows, I'm not moving all that fast. My legs are gone, and trembling willow branches have taken their places. The saplings serve to move me around, but they are too unsteady to serve me well. I yearn to sit on the floor, stretch out, and curl small, so Mr. Godbold could never find me. *"Where's that girl Pauline? What's become of her? Where did she get to? Did anyone see her leave?"*

Ah, and I would laugh in my hiding place. How I would laugh that he could not discover me. I might be a piece of lint, so that he would walk right past me. The floor would rumble beneath me, and I would sleep, my fingers rid of their cramps; my shoulders, their knots. My eyelids drag as if they would close, but I cannot sleep, for the whistle has not called, has not wailed.

The bobbins whirl. Do they never get tired? No, just fatter, so Jimmy has to leap for them and put in more to feed. They are never satisfied, these bobbins.

A scream rings out close by. I feel a rush of air by my face and a thud on my foot.

When I look down, Jimmy has crumpled atop my leg, his weight on my foot, pinning me to the floor. I do not want to kick him off, so I push and roll him over. His eyes are closed, and his mouth twists to one side as if the screams have fled, leaving him empty.

I shout to be heard. "Get up, Jimmy! Get up off my foot! You're hurting me!"

I push him again, nudge him away, angry he does not answer or open his eyes. My ankle aches with the load of him. I want to take off my shoe and sock to console my foot. *Poor thing. Don't cry.*

Jimmy raises one arm to reach for his other hand beneath him. He grimaces, contorting his face, but I cannot hear the scream. It must be stuck in his throat.

When I look down at the hand he cradles, something is missing. White bone glares like a naked truth, like a streak of pure lightning in a dark sky.

A spasm shakes my chest. My mouth goes dry, and the taste of cabbage rises in my throat. I swallow hard to force my dinner back down before I scream as loud as I can. "Mr. Godbold! Mr. Godbold, come quick! The spinner has taken his thumb!"

Blood drips onto the thundering floor, seeping into Jimmy's blue sleeve.

M<small>ISS</small> <small>BERTHA'S</small> <small>SATCHEL</small> holds many things. When she laid it open to get that knife, I saw a ball of twine, a packet of dried leaves, her snuff, and scissors. She brings the rolled-up packet and a square of flimsy cloth to me.

"Here," she says. "Find a cup."

I reach into the cupboard, grabbing one I had just dried and put away. It has a bluebird on it and what I think used to be pink roses. They are faded now, so that the bird and the flowers seem a dream.

"Will this do?"

"Good," Miss Bertha says. "Good." She looks around the stove room. "You've washed up everything. Good." Her face wrinkles more when she smiles. Grasping the small square of gauze, she dumps a handful of the dried leaves onto it, and with a flick of her gnarled fingers, she twists the gauze closed and places the bundle in the cup. She ladles in boiling water from the stove.

We watch as the tan seeps into the water.

"Blue cohosh," she says. "Squash vine and raspberry leaf, with a touch of mint. It'll bring her along faster and stronger. I only wish we had some honey."

I shrug. "There's some sorghum."

"No, I think not. In a little while you might want to see about Percy. His mama says he's sleeping." She rolls the packet back up. "And the washpot out back. We'll need a fire to boil the rags later."

I start to go, but Miss Bertha hovers over the teacup. She looks up at me, her black eyes probing my face. I want to look away, but her gaze holds me. "It doesn't seem that long since you and Pauline were borned." She cackles. "I didn't know there was two of you. A fine joke on me. A fine joke on everybody, even your mama."

I smell the tea steeping, sharp like the peppermint drops in the glass jars at the company store. "A 'joke'?"

She nods. "Yes. When your daddy come home—he was working night shift then—he was half asleep in the early morning." She raises her hands before her. "There the two of you was, sleeping aside your mama—two little pert rosebuds, pink and warm. He blinked, and then he blinked again."

The odor of peppermint grows stronger, and the raspberry smells like the berries on summer bushes. *A joke?*

"Then he set down in the chair next the bed and dropped his head." Miss Bertha smiles, the crinkles deep around her eyes. "He said to your mama, 'Mother, there are two?' Your mama nodded. Then he said low as I could hardly not hear him, 'Mother, we are undone! We are ruined!' "

" 'Ruined'?"

She laughs. "Guess he wondered how he could feed two more mouths." She picks up the cup. "This is ready now. I'll take it to her. She needs it for her strength."

I take the soggy bag she lifts out, the heat of it burning my hand. I want to ask who came first. *Was it me or Pauline? Who was the one too many?*

In my heart I know the answer. *A fine baby girl! Oh no—there's another one. We are ruined.*

I pick up the pail again. It will take at least four more trips to the pump to fill the black iron pot out back. My shoulders suffer already, and I think of the stove room at home growing cold, the dinner pots white with grease, and the wash grown stiff on the line. I've had no dinner, and my stomach growls in protest, rumbling at me.

The afternoon has turned gray, and my thinking turns to Pauline at the mill, warm with her friends, Mama, Daddy, and Josh close by, and I wonder if this day will ever end.

SIX

THE SUPERVISOR, who is usually at my shoulder, is nowhere to be seen. I shout again, "Mr. Godbold!" I call so loud, I feel my chest empty and my breath rush in, full of the stale-cotton air.

One of the sweeping boys turns, dropping his broom as he starts toward me. When he gets near, he freezes, his eyes on Jimmy and the oozing blood.

I scream at him. "Edwin, don't just stand there like a jackass! Get Mr. Godbold!"

Still he roots in the spot like he has forgotten how to move. I would reach down to shift Jimmy off my foot so I can go, but I cannot bring myself to lay a hand on him. I might touch the blood. My foot is numb from Jimmy's weight. I try to wiggle my toes, but I cannot.

Edwin looks up, his eyes staring through me. Only his hand works at his side. He folds his thumb in—the one he likes to suck—and wraps his other fingers over it so that his hand balls into a fist.

You would think I am the only real person here. Jimmy and Edwin have turned to statues. "Mr. Godbold!" The bobbins twirl. I reach out to slap Edwin hard. The blow connects to Edwin's hard little shoulder and stings my hand.

Edwin continues to gaze at me as if he cannot figure out where the blow came from. Perhaps he thinks what struck out at Jimmy has also hit him. At length he gathers himself, dashing off beyond our row.

Perhaps if I yell loud enough, will Mama come?
No, she is so far down the room, she won't hear. I'll
pretend I'm Arlene. My foot! My foot, Mama! Come
get Jimmy off my foot.

But it is Mr. Godbold who comes, with
Edwin close behind. Mr. Godbold's right eye
finds us, and he turns to shoo Edwin away.
Pretty soon two more men come. Together
they lift Jimmy up and carry him away, his
bare feet dangling like a rag doll's.

I flex my foot and take a quick step. It
feels like wood, the toes all one solid piece,
like a block. The bobbins call to me: *You must*
wait. You must wait for the monkey-faced Jimmy.
He will come soon and clamber to you, his mouth
untwisted and grinning. You wait. But they do not
stop. They keep on filling up. Their hunger
drives them like gluttons.

Edwin comes to stand beside me, his face
eager. He shouts over the noise. "I can do it!
I can do Jimmy's job."

He is too short. I challenge him. "Did Mr. Godbold say?"

He shakes his head. "No." His dimples give him a Christmas-cherub look. He is small for seven, and peaked.

I shake my head back at him. We have to yell. "Then you shan't."

He insists. "Yes, I can."

"You're a sweeper, not a doffer."

"Watch me." He pulls off his shoes and kicks them aside. He throws his socks in a heap. Inches shorter than Jimmy, he stretches for the first rung up the machine. I do not want to watch, but I have to. He clings with his feet, thrusting his body up, his fingers extended until he connects with the bobbin, sliding it down as he balances on his toes, white where they bend. The soles of his feet are as dark as the floor.

He drops down, bearing the full bobbin, stretching again to replace it. I cannot watch anymore. I turn away. *What about you, poor foot?* I limp a few steps. I have no pain, only a curious lack of feeling, when I mount to the broken threads.

Mr. Godbold comes back, eyeing Edwin's climb and my tying. He says nothing. A spot of red stains the front of his shirt. I guess it to be Jimmy's blood, wrung by the machine. Mr. Godbold moves Edwin's broom over to the corner and props it against the wall.

Jimmy's fall and my foot have wakened me. I am alert to several threads now. A strange thought enters my head. *What of Jimmy's thumb? He will not see it again until Judgment Day.*

THE FIRE SPRINGS to life under the old iron pot, making it look like a black devil hunkering down in the orange flames. The sky has turned to gray flannel, darker than before, but pink streaks it in places, and I smell ice in the air.

The last time I passed the bedroom, Mrs. Harrell lay quiet, and Miss Bertha dozed in the chair, her hands crossed on her chest, her head tilted over on one shoulder. She was up much of the night, she said, with Miss Louise's daughter, who has measles and pneumonia. She put tar packs and Vicks salve on the girl's chest. She said the girl's breathing sounded like a saw drawn across tin.

When I've made the fire and gone back inside, I hear Mrs. Harrell. "Ah-a-a-a-a-h! Ah-a-a-a-a-h!"

"That's right," comes old Bertha's voice. "Keep it low. Low tones do the work faster."

I go in search of Percy, but he is not sleeping, rather crouching by his narrow cot. I touch him lightly on the shoulder. He starts like he did not hear me come into the room. I stoop to him. "Percy?"

He waddles two steps away from me, clenching his hands to his knees. I reach out and pull him to me. Sidling away he whimpers, "Ma-ma."

"Your mama's all right. It's just that you're going to get a new brother or sister." But what's that to him? He's still a baby himself.

As I lift him up I feel the dampness of his rompers. Where are the diapers? A stack of clean linens lies at the foot of the cot. As I strip off the wet cloth, he studies me, his dark eyes serious with curiosity. *Who are you?* he seems to ask. *Who are you? Why are you here?*

"Did you sleep well?" I ask.

I slide the dry cloth under him, careful to put my finger between him and the pin as I fasten the diaper. I have to push hard to get the pin through the fabric. *It needs soap,* I think. Mama would rub all the pins on a bar of sweet soap to make them slide through easier. It is cold in the room, and I hurry to finish dressing Percy and get him to the warmth. I hear Mrs. Harrell again, and Percy jerks his head toward the door, frowning, his upper lip quivering.

"Are you hungry?" I know not to expect an answer.

I pick him up to take him, squirming, to the stove room. His hands are icy at the back of my neck. He lays his head down briefly before a searing pain shoots through my shoulder. He has bitten me! My first impulse is to pop his leg, but I restrain myself, plopping him down in a chair at the table.

"No," I tell him. "That was very bad." I want to tell him that one does not bite the hands that intend to feed him, but I know I would be wasting my breath.

Rifling through the cupboard, I find the cornmeal, and in a box on the back porch I see butter, eggs, and a jug of milk. I set about making corn bread. It will not put flesh on his bones, but it will stay the hunger for a while.

Oh, for my own dinner on the back of the cold stove at home, but I can't leave this tyke—not with Miss Bertha, and Mrs. Harrell close to her time.

He watches as I mix up the batter and pour it into the skillet. I move one of the water pots aside. I do not understand Miss Bertha's need of all the water. It is enough for Saturday baths for us all.

I sit opposite Percy while the hoecake cooks, watching him sniff the air like a small furry fox. Each time we hear Mrs. Harrell, he makes a move as if he would get down from the table to go to her, but he seems afraid. Resting his hands on the table, he looks resigned, like a little old man, but he continues to eye the stove and me.

When I go back out on the porch for his milk, I hear a fine scattering, like someone is wrinkling tissue paper somewhere a long way away or like the sound of corn hitting the ground in the chicken yard. It is sleet falling, whirled by the wind.

I set a cup of milk before Percy and slice

the round of yellow bread like a pie before I lift out a piece to lather with butter. My mouth waters, but it is not my food, my house. I only lick my fingers after I set the bread down before him.

His hands fly to it.

"Hot!" I say. "Hot, very hot!"

He touches it anyway, drawing back his fingers and sticking them into his mouth.

Miss Bertha comes to the door. "Come quick! I need your help."

SEVEN

MORE THAN LIKELY, Mama will do a pounding for Jimmy, like she and the other ladies always do when times are hard. They will go through their larders to find a pound or two of this or that to take over to the family. I know when Margaret's mother had pneumonia and could not work, they kept a steady stream of things going in her door.

But that was summertime, when sweet corn tasseled fat in rows out back and green beans plumped on vines. Someone even made a berry pie, its crust sugary and purple. Margaret's daddy did not mind the charity.

"It burns me up," my daddy said. "That drone of a man. What kind of man is that with a sick wife and four girls working? He doesn't do a lick of work." Daddy rapped his knuckles on the table. "He oughta be horse-whipped."

Mama turned her head, lifting her chin. "The girls shouldn't be made to suffer because of him."

Daddy looked down at the greens Mama was wrapping for the pounding. "But he puts his feet under the table as well."

"It rains on the just and unjust alike," Mama said, pursing her lips.

"Scripture doesn't make it right."

Jimmy's pounding will be different. Maybe a lump of butter, some white eggs from our brown hen, and a quart of milk from Widow Wade's cow. Perhaps some will bring rice, or dried beans still hard in their skins. People might give a piece of salt pork from the fall slaughter, when the men dressed the hams, if any is left. Jimmy picked the wrong time of year to hurt himself. Food is not so plentiful now, or cheap if you must buy it.

Autumn is the best time here. Mama cooks a pork roast and bakes sweet potatoes so good you burn your fingers to get to the sweetness. And the weather is fine. We have cool nights and blue-sky days. It is not so dark in the morning or early night. Sometimes after supper we jump rope or play tag or snake in the gutter, the street full of us.

But here in the spinning room—fall, winter, spring, or summer—it is always August, with the machines making thunder, promising rain, but the rain never comes, only heat and more promises.

The light from the windows grows dimmer. I have to bend closer to see the threads. I do not believe an hour still remains of the day. Mr. Godbold roams but says little, only takes out his watch, looks at it, and frowns. I should like to know how close the hand has come to six o'clock, how many more minutes until the whistle weeps its last for me, until time to go home.

As I near my house, I will see the lamps burning, smell biscuits baking when I come in the door, with maybe a curl of ham and syrup or sorghum or honey. Sweet milk will fill my cup.

I think ahead to take my mind off my foot. The numbness has gone, and it throbs. My shoe is too tight. I would like to take it off, but a voice whispers to me: *Leave it on. Keep it on for now. The road is cold on the way home. When you're safe there, it will be time enough.*

Ah, the whistle. My sweater. Edwin drops to the floor to put on his shoes and socks. We press to the door.

Mr. Godbold stops me, catches me by the shoulder, and leans close to my ear. "You have a sister. Isn't Arlene her name?"

I nod.

"We will be short a sweeper tomorrow. Edwin will take Jimmy's place. Have Arlene come in to work."

I start to protest. *Her foot. It is all because of her foot she doesn't work. She could not climb to the threads.* Sweeping—that is boys' work. But I do not say anything to Mr. Godbold. It will serve her right. My sister, the petted one, will learn what it's like to work.

I GLANCE BACK AT PERCY. He is stuffing his mouth with corn bread as I follow Miss Bertha back to the front room.

She has lined the bed with newspaper, and Mrs. Harrell lies there with her nightdress up over her thighs. I should think her chilled in this cold room, but sweat plasters fine strands of hair to her forehead and shines on her arms and knees. The room smells of perspiration and faintly of mint.

"It's time," Miss Bertha says again. "Put your hand on her belly, and when I tell her to push, bear down on her."

I do as she says, and the belly feels full and tight but greasy from some kind of salve, and my hand slips. Mrs. Harrell whimpers.

"Push, dearie. Push hard."

Mrs. Harrell pants and mutters, "I can't. I can't."

Miss Bertha peers between Mrs. Harrell's legs. "Just a little bit more. Just a bit more. Just a little bit."

But Mrs. Harrell does not respond, only flings her hand across her face. I stand there, wishing I were home, hating the feel of her belly and the sound of the rustling newspaper. I despise touching what does not belong to me and am ashamed for her somehow.

Fixing her beady black eyes on me, Miss Bertha wipes her own forehead. "She is tuckered out, but it's too soon to rest." She upbraids Mrs. Harrell in a stern voice.

"Frances, don't fight me on this. You still have work to do. There'll be time to rest when you're done."

Her words seem harsh, but they don't faze Mrs. Harrell, whose eyes are closed and teeth clenched. I worry about Percy in there with the hot stove. I want to go see about him, but I dare not leave.

Miss Bertha stoops for her satchel and pulls out her scissors, twine, and her box of snuff. I do not understand. She can't be looking to dip snuff now—but sure enough, she takes off the lid and grabs a generous pinch. She does not put it to her mouth but carries it to Mrs. Harrell's face. She stops, her hand in midair. "Be ready to bear down," she says to me.

What is she going to do? I watch, fixed, as Miss Bertha puts the snuff to Mrs. Harrell's nose, coaxing the brown powder into the nostrils. Mrs. Harrell opens her eyes to stare straight ahead before she inhales sharply, rubbing her nose. "KER-CHOO! KER-CHOO! KER-CHOO!" Mrs. Harrell sneezes, startling me, but I push down anyway.

"That's it! That's it!" Miss Bertha cackles, her face collapsed into a smile. She snatches up a rag and lapses into baby talk. "Got to give it some air, wipe its little mouth and nose."

I look down at the stained newspaper to see a dark head emerging, its hair like fur in the rain. Miss Bertha tugs. "Push easy. Yes, that's it. Just look at you. There, there." She lifts the child slightly and raises her hand.

I hear a slap and then an outraged howl. I peek a look at the little face screwed up, red and angry. *Welcome. It won't always be so bad. You'll have some good times, too.*

"It's a boy," Miss Bertha says. "A hefty

one at that. Have you picked out a name, Frances? Have you a boy's name ready?"

Mrs. Harrell shakes her head before she turns her eyes to the wall. Miss Bertha sends me with the scissors to the boiling water. *Someday I will be able to say, "I was there the afternoon you were born. I saw you first. Sleet fell that afternoon in January." But I will not tell him that when he was born, his mother turned her face to the wall.*

EIGHT

I IS ALMOST DARK OUTSIDE, and icy particles whirl in the air.

Mama jostles my arm as we fall into step, but I am limping.

"Pauline?"

I try to make my foot cooperate, but it will not do as I say. It wants to quit this far from home, for me to lie down. I step on it as little as possible, doing a quick hop to the other one.

Katie and Margaret go skipping by. One calls, "Pauline, is that you?"

Pulling my sweater to me, I feel the cold

seek out the dampness of my dress again, and icy flecks pelt my face. The cold eases the foot's throbbing but bites at my cheeks.

Daddy and Josh join us, moving ahead, Josh's cap pulled down, his head ducked to the wind. I hobble as fast as I can.

Josh looks back. "Pauline, that you?"

Who do they think I am—Arlene?

Mama's dinner bucket bangs mine. There be time for talk at home, time over hot buttered biscuits and sweet milk. Now I must get there. I will myself along, one step leading to another, each step one step nearer home, but the road grows slick, and I feel my foot slide a little before I catch myself.

I strain my eyes to see, seeking out our house in the failing light. I'll find it and fasten my eyes on it. *It will reel me to it like the bobbins.*

But which is ours? No lantern glows there, no brightness at all. It must be I am thinking only of my foot or the frosty air. I blink, but still I see no light.

As we get closer, Mama exclaims, "No light! By now Arlene would have lighted the lamp. No smoke from the chimney, either."

Aha, lazy sister. This time we have caught you. This time we will catch you sleeping, curled up under the quilt. Mama will rant. Daddy will scowl, and you, the favored one, will wilt from their scorn. We are hungry and tired and cold. We'll get you this time.

"She must be sick," Mama says.

I gloat, sure of what we will find. My anger and feeling of triumph carry me the rest of the way through the icy rain, the cold sliding down the back of my neck.

Daddy and Josh have already bounded the steps. The door stands wide.

Mama and I follow, Mama calling, "Arlene! Arlene?"

Wanting to be the first to find her, I go straight to our room, but the bed is spread, the covers tucked. In the dusk I can see her pillow—hers and mine, just so.

After lighting the wick, Mama replaces the smoky shade. "She hasn't cleaned the lamp." The light shows the greasy dinner pots, the empty biscuit pan. She peers out back. "The wash is still on the line."

My stomach churns with emptiness. I sink down in a chair at the table and reach to take off my shoe to inspect my foot. No one notices. I rub it, trying to coax it to feel better. Mama sends Josh to the pump and Daddy out for wood.

The lantern gathers more light, and Mama frowns as she lifts the pots from the stove to the sink. "Her dinner's still here on the stove. Something has happened, I know."

Daddy comes in, his arms full of wood. Sleet glistens in his hair like bright lint.

No, Arlene didn't eat her dinner. She probably filled her stomach on sweets at the company store. No poor plain food for her.

Josh stamps his feet before he bangs through the front door with the pail. He puts it down and rubs his hands together.

"Well," Mama says, "somebody's sick, I wager. The child will be home before long."

"Want me to go ask around?" Josh asks.

"No, Josh. She'll be home directly. Then we'd have to look for you."

Daddy strikes a match. Drops fall from his hair.

"Frances Harrell may be having her baby, and Arlene is over there." Mama fills the stove pot with water.

"No," Daddy says, closing the stove. "Sam Harrell stopped off from work at the store. He was in no hurry to get home."

Maybe she's gossiping there. Full of sweets, she's listening to talk, standing around in the store.

Daddy sits at the table, rubbing his eyes. "I don't like what happened today. I don't like what it means. It means trouble."

Mama scoops lard into a bowl. "'Trouble'? I know what happened to poor Jimmy. Is that what you're meaning to say?"

"No, people snooping around, nosing around in other folks' business. Folks—strangers taking pictures. They mean to cause trouble." He wipes his nose on the back of his sleeve. "They would stop us from working our own young'uns in the mill. *Our* young'uns—as if they belonged to somebody else."

Frowning, Mama says, "Pauline, go bring in the wash."

Don't they know my shoulders ache, that my foot beats like it has a heart of its own? "I have my shoe off."

Daddy glowers. "You heard your mama! Put your shoe on again."

But I can't. I can only get my toes in. I half drag my shoe as I clomp down the steps into the cold, stretching for the stiff wash.

I have not told them yet that Arlene must go to work tomorrow. I will not tell them until she comes home. I will wait and heap more shame on her head.

ALTHOUGH THE BABY has arrived, Miss Bertha has no end of things for me to do. After she's tied and cut the cord, she sets the child aside and turns her attention back to Mrs. Harrell.

"The afterbirth comes easy," she says to me.

She sends me for a basin of hot water and more cloth squares. Wadding up the soiled newspapers from the bed, she hands them to me. "Put these in the fire out back."

The wind blows in as I push open the door. As I cram the papers under the old iron pot, the fire springs to life, sending up sparks like red fireflies. I think it is still sleeting, but the wind scatters everything.

When I go back through the stove room, Percy sits at the table, most of his corn bread gone, but he hunts down every crumb, seeks each out with his thumb and forefinger, aiming it for his mouth. A milk line rings his upper lip. I smile at him to reassure him, but he focuses only on the next crumb.

I do not see a clock anywhere, and the gray afternoon gives me no idea of the time. I cannot trust my growling stomach, either, for it is long past the dinner hour. The messy stove room at home calls me. *Arlene! Arlene, come home!* And the widow's cow. If I don't do the milking tonight, everyone will be angry. But Miss Bertha still has need of me.

Miss Bertha has spread out the baby's arms to sponge him, wringing the cloth over the basin. "Look in the chest at the foot of Percy's bed. Frances says you will find the young'un's things."

Lifting the trunk lid I find a pile of soft clothes, a faded pink silk rose, and the family bible bound in black. I feel I am meddling in things that are not mine when I take up one of the baby gowns. You would think it's been washed at least a hundred times. You can tell where the tatting had pulled away at the neck, then was mended in fine, even stitches. I take up a shawl, too, crocheted of ivory wool, and head back. Miss Bertha has finished bathing the child and reaches for the clothes.

He seems troubled to be naked, and bothered as she pats him dry. He scrunches up his forehead. His fingers tighten around his thumbs, and he flails his arms and whimpers. *It's all right. She's almost done.*

In one motion Miss Bertha opens the gown, slipping it over his head and inserting his arms. She lays the shawl flat to bring up one corner over his feet; the side points she folds around his body. "There. You're cozy again."

She turns to me. "Fetch a lamp. We'll be needing it soon so a body can see. And some tea." She glances over at Mrs. Harrell. "Frances could use another cup and so could I." She gathers together her snuff, scissors, and twine, and retrieves her knife from under the bed.

When I return with the two cups, she has changed Mrs. Harrell's nightdress, adding it to the soiled cloths piled on the floor.

Miss Bertha points to the stack. "These need to be put in the washpot. Stir them down good with a stick."

I report to the bedroom for more orders

to find Mrs. Harrell lying propped on a pillow, the quilt spread over her. She sips her tea, pausing to blow on it. "This is good and hot."

Miss Bertha holds her cup in her crooked fingers, the steam rising in her face. Percy has crept to the doorway, his eyes wide in the lamplight.

A knock comes at the door. It's too soon for anyone visiting. The mill hasn't let out. There has been no hoot of the whistle.

It's Matt Withely, his red hair wild and mixed with lint and sleet. He doesn't bother with a greeting. "Is the granny woman here? Miss Bertha—is she here?"

I nod.

"Tell her to come quick," Matt says. "There's been an accident over to the mill. It's Jimmy."

Miss Bertha has heard. She gathers up her satchel and slings on her jacket. Turning to me she says, "Things should probably be all right. Just stay with them until Sam comes home." She starts to go but turns back. "If you could catch up on Frances's wash and ironing, I know she'd be much obliged."

I think of the iron pot out in the yard and all the wash cooking like the devil's foul stew, and I wonder how long the day must go on, how many hours it takes to make up the day.

Pauline, your work is soon done. The owl will hoot, and you will say good night to Katie and Margaret, and I still have supper to get and no friends to tell good-bye. Oh, Pauline, the perfect one. Pauline, the firstborn perfect one.

NINE

THE FLATIRON HEATS on the stove.

Mama has washed up the dinner pots and hands me a towel to dry them. I would just like to sit and coddle my foot.

Mama speaks to Daddy. "We'll put off supper awhile. We'll wait 'til Arlene comes home. She can't be long now. Pauline can finish the ironing."

Of course we cannot have our supper until Arlene comes. Of course. Why must I do the ironing? Let the lazy one do it when she comes—she who has done nothing all afternoon except lounge, and stuff on sweets.

I spread a quilt on the table and unfold

Daddy's overalls, then drop them in favor of Josh's shirt, easier to press. Ire rises in me. This is not my job. I *work*. These clothes belong at the foot of the bed when we come home at night, creased and folded and smelling of strong soap.

"Test the iron first, Pauline," Mama says. "It may not be hot enough."

Taking it up I touch my finger to the bottom of it. "Ouch!"

"Not like that, Pauline." Mama dips her fingers in the water and flicks drops at the iron. The water skitters and slides, sizzling. "Yes," Mama says. "It's hot aplenty."

While I drag the heavy iron over Josh's clothes, Mama hauls out a bag of flour and goes outside for the milk.

When she comes back she is shaking her head. "I can't understand what's keeping Arlene. Might could be she went over to help with Jimmy."

"Jimmy was hurt late this afternoon." An edge creeps into my voice. "It's plain she's not been here since dinnertime."

"That's true," Mama says, frowning. "And the sleet is worse now. When I went out back, you could hear it clicking on the roof." She shakes her head. "She'll be slow and cold coming home."

Why does Mama worry about Arlene? *What about me, Mama? I am tired to the very insides of my bones, and my foot has turned blue on the top. And you fret over Arlene.*

"Josh?" Mama goes to the hall, calling for him.

I hear the bedsprings creak.

Josh sticks his head around the door. "Yes, Mama?"

"I don't know what I was thinking. If Arlene hasn't been home, she hasn't done the milking, and Widow Wade is ailing." She glances around. "No, of course not. There's the milk can." Flour covers Mama's hands. "Go do it quick. That cow will be bawling by now." She works the dough, her hands pumping up and down. "That's the least we can do since the widow shares the milk with us."

Josh screws up his mouth. I can tell he doesn't want to go out in the cold to milk the cow, but he knows better than to give Mama sass. Daddy has a razor strop he is not afraid to use.

Most of the wrinkles have lain flat, except for the mended sleeve. I think of Jimmy's blue sleeve, the blood soaking in like ink into a blotter. I hand the shirt over. "Here, Josh."

He takes it and looks down. "Arlene usually folds it."

"This is not Arlene," I want to say, but I catch myself. Mama is watching.

"Be quick about it," she tells him. "We'll have supper soon. And mind you, don't leave the calf with her too long. There'll be nothing but blue john left."

The shirts are finished, and I am left with the overalls, stiff and unwieldy. They have a mind of their own. While I wait for the iron to heat again, I watch Mama roll out the dough and, taking up an old tin cup, ring it in flour before cutting the biscuits out to lay them on the black baking tin. She puts a slice of ham cut five ways into the skillet. The kitchen fills with the smell of it, making my mouth water.

I hobble into Mama's room with the overalls. Daddy lies on the bed, his shoes beside, his arm draped over his face. If he's asleep, I don't want to waken him. I leave the overalls and steal away. *Would you thank me, Daddy, if you were not sleeping? Would you say, "I know how weary you are, as tired as I and yet you ironed my clothes"?* Somehow I know he would not. I am not his precious Arlene.

THE LIGHT GROWS DIM as I pin up the rest of the wash. I turn back to see the clothes-line, the cloths and nightdress like ghosts of the afternoon past. The sleet hisses in the fire. It whines: *Be quiet. What have you to complain of?* Oh, the whistle blows. I shall be going home soon, as soon as Mr. Harrell comes from work. I hurry in, my fingers wrinkled and numb from the water and cold, my chin and cheeks blocks of ice. My nose runs. I sniffle. I know the wash will freeze on the line tonight, but at least it is clean.

What a comfort the stove room is after the bluster outside! Only one small crumb escaped Percy's hunt, but I wipe the table anyway. Once Miss Bertha spreads the word, the ladies will come with pots of beans, a dried-apple pie, or potatoes roasted in their skins. Everything must be tidy. There's Percy's milk cup on the table and the tea mugs in the bedroom. I go to fetch them.

Mrs. Harrell dozes, the baby grown quiet at the foot of the bed. Percy has crept into the chair, watching them like a cat eyeing a family of mice—like he would pounce at the slightest movement. Miss Bertha's cup is cold but half filled.

What happened to Jimmy?

She stirs. "Hand me the baby, Arlene." She sits up and holds out her arms.

Percy watches as I put down the cup and slide one hand under the bundle's bottom, the other under its head. The child's warmth is surprising, radiating from him through the shawl, but he is as light as a packet of fluff. I place him in her hands and move the lamp closer so the light plays on them both.

She looks down in his face. "He is like Percy. They're as alike as two peas in a pod." She traces a finger along his face. "Even the way his eyebrows grow." She looks at me and smiles. "I think I shall name him Aaron, after my father."

Aaron. Aaron and Percy. Arlene and Pauline. Alike as two peas in a pod.

Mrs. Harrell studies his face a few moments before she asks, "The whistle? Has it sounded?"

"Yes," I answer.

"Sam will be coming home soon." She curves the baby's fingers over her hand. "My first one was stillborn, a boy. When Percy was born, Sam was proud to have him a son. He'll be surprised. This time we thought certain it was a girl."

Another just the same. Was she disappointed the same?

I take the cups out back to wash up, listening for Mr. Harrell, but I hear only the sleet, like a clock ticking, only the hum of the fire. I add a stick of wood. How I long for my supper, my bed!

Pauline and Josh, Mama and Daddy are home by now, home to the cheerless house, where nothing cooks, where greasy pots greet them, but they are home, not tied to a sleet-bound house down the road.

Still no Mr. Harrell. I have to keep moving, else I will fall asleep. I have not asked Mrs. Harrell if she would like anything to eat. But what is there? I could at least put on a pot of beans. Yes, they are filling—that and the corn bread.

It grows dark. I peer into the night in vain. I see no one coming down the road. Mrs. Harrell puts the baby to her breast, and Percy clambers onto the bed, trying to climb into her lap.

"He's not been weaned so long ago him-self that he doesn't remember," she says.

I reach out to take Percy.

Mrs. Harrell raises her hand. "No, never mind. He shall have to get used to his little brother. This is Aaron, Percy."

Percy shoves as if he would topple the baby from her arms.

A clatter sounds out on the stoop, and the front door bursts open, swirling cold air in from the hall. Mr. Harrell stomps into the room, his face red, his boots rimmed in ice. He smells of beer.

He is tall, his arms so long that his sleeves dangle unbuttoned at the wrists. "It's come, has it?"

"Yes," says Mrs. Harrell. "Where have you been?" The baby makes a snuffling noise as she waits for an answer.

Mr. Harrell runs a hand through his wet hair. "I had no dinner at noon. I stopped by the store." He scowls. "A man can't work on breakfast alone." He gestures to the baby. "What is it?"

"Another boy," she says.

"Humph. I believe boys is all that's in you."

Mother, we are undone. We are ruined.

I go to the stove room to get my sweater. He follows me there and lifts the lid of the bean pot. Before I can stop him, he dips in the spoon and lifts it to his mouth. He blows hard on it and pops a few beans in, but he only chews a few seconds before he spits out his mouthful. "They are raw," he says.

"I only just put them on a half hour ago. They have not finished cooking. There's sweet milk out back and corn bread."

His breath is sour, his eyes ringed in red. He glowers at me. "A man works all day for corn bread and milk. What kind of house is this?"

I don't answer, knowing I have nothing to say. Besides, at last I can go home.

TEN

WHEN THE DOOR CLOSES, Mama jumps up. "Oh, Arlene. Where have you been? I've been worried sick about you."

I dry the last dish and put it away in the cupboard. It clinks on the stack.

Mama helps Arlene off with her sweater. "Where in the world have you been?" She shakes the sweater, making the droplets splatter the floor, and drapes the woolen over a chair by the stove.

"Mrs. Harrell had her baby this afternoon. Miss Bertha found me after the dinner pails, on my way home. 'I'll need help,' she said to me, and I went with her."

"I thought as much. You must be nearly frozen. Sit down by the fire. Have you had supper?"

"No, Mama. I made some corn bread and set on a pot of beans, but they hadn't cooked, not yet."

I feel invisible. Arlene is the only one here.

"Is the baby all right?" Mama asks.

"Yes, Mama. Another boy."

"And Mrs. Harrell?"

"She does well. Miss Bertha was called to see about Jimmy. I had to wait for Mr. Harrell to come home." Arlene shivers and rubs her shoulder. "How is Jimmy? What happened?"

"He lost a finger. He'll be all right. Give his hand a chance to mend." She gestures to Arlene. "Sit down. I'll get you something to eat." She frowns at me. "Move, Pauline. Let your sister sit there by the fire."

Daddy comes in. "Arlene?"

"Yes, Arlene is home. I was right. Frances Harrell's time had come. She's been over helping Miss Bertha." Mama wipes out the sink with her rag. "It's just biscuits and ham. Shall I get it for you?"

"No, Mama. I'll fix it," Arlene says.

I want to shout, "The laundry is done, the dishes washed—your jobs." But I wait for the time. When shall I tell her? *Your days of lollygagging with the neighbors are over. You must work tomorrow, Mr. Godbold says.*

She will find out what real work is all about. Mama keeps fussing over her, and I, whose foot throbs and whose head aches, keep quiet.

Limping around the table, I pull out another chair and sit, waiting for the time. You'd think they'd notice how I have to walk. I should like to say, "Look at my foot. Come see my poor foot. Feel how weary I am," but I can't because no one looks in my direction. They center everything on Arlene.

Mama glows as Arlene takes up her biscuit. "Has the weather worsened?"

Arlene nods, her mouth full.

"Ethel said Carrie and George ran away this afternoon to get married but turned back because of the ice." Mama pours out a cup of milk, putting it before the spoiled sister. Mama straightens up and shakes her head. "'Tis an ill wind that doesn't blow somebody good. At least they were kept from it for today."

"They're hardheaded," Daddy says. "But even if they have to wait 'til spring, they'll find a way."

Mama looks over at him. "*We* did."

Daddy looks around the stove room. His glance lingers on each of us a moment. "We did. Yes, we did."

He goes out back, coming in with wood. "I'll bank the fire before I go to bed."

Now is the time. I only wish Josh were here, that he hadn't already gone to bed. "Tomorrow, Arlene must go to work."

Mama frowns. "'To work'? What do you mean?"

Ah, yes. Your precious Arlene. How do you like that? "Yes, she must go to the mill."

Daddy looks puzzled.

I have their attention.

Her forehead stays wrinkled. "But why?"

I hold out one more minute before I say, "Mr. Godbold says."

"But her foot," Mama says. "She can't reach and can't climb to the threads. Besides, the spinners are covered."

The moment tastes good. I roll it around in my mouth. "Edwin will be doffer while Jimmy is gone. Mr. Godbold needs Arlene to sweep." I watch their faces. "I'm sure she can manage *that*."

Arlene smiles. "Oh yes! I can manage that."

Her smile puzzles me.

LYING AWAKE I LISTEN to hear if the sleet still clicks on the house. I hear nothing but the wind. And over it the sound of the whistle, jerky, uncertain, like the owl has hiccups today.

Mama stands above us, already fully dressed. "Get up, Pauline. It's time, Arlene. Don't even try the privy this morning. Use the slop jar instead."

Usually Mama hates for us to use it, knowing we sometimes forget to empty it. "Why?"

"The snow," she answers. "When I went out, I bogged down up to my knees. The sleet changed to snow during the night. Your daddy hasn't time to shovel it away from the outhouse now."

Pauline props up on one elbow. "Will the mill open?"

Mama snorts. "What does the mill know of snow? It knows only cotton. Hurry. Breakfast is almost done."

The room is cold, and the chamber pot colder when I fetch it from under the bed. I throw on my clothes in the dark. Pauline has risen and used the pot. Out of habit, I reach down to pull up the covers and plump up the pillows, but it is hard to see what is straight.

Pauline has on her clothes and sits in a chair to pull on her socks and shoes. "Oh no."

"What is wrong?" I ask.

"My shoe won't go on."

She mocks me, I know, as I tie the laces

on Josh's shoe. I know she is jealous I get to go to work, too, but I will not let her bother me. "Well, the other one of Josh's pair is there. There, under the bed. Try that."

I go in to help Mama ladle out the oatmeal.

"Get the milk, Arlene."

Stepping out back I find the wind has stilled. The milk has frozen, has pushed its way up like something climbing out of a well. The top sits up high, a hat. "Look, Mama."

She hands me a bowl and a spoon. "Try scraping some off the top."

I grate the spoon across. Fine slivers flake into the bowl until it is half full. I take it in and go back for more.

Josh already sits at the table, looking down at his oatmeal. "I shoveled the front, Mama, as much as I could see to do. It won't be bad—at least to the road."

The pails sit out, and I wonder: *Only four, but five of us go to work. Who will bring dinner if I am already at the mill?*

Mama reads my mind. "You and Pauline will share a bucket today. There's no help for it."

While she waits for Daddy to come in for breakfast, Mama splits biscuits and puts a small piece of ham in each. "It's not a proper dinner, but we'll have to take it along with us when we go. There'll be no one to fetch it to us at work."

How selfish I am. So glad am I to go to work, and the others will suffer because of it.

Mama calls to Daddy and Pauline. "Breakfast! Hurry!"

Pauline comes in frowning. She takes a quick step, and her shoe clunks. She is wearing Josh's other old shoe after all. She all but trips over it.

This is no time for tricks. We have no time for

games, Pauline. Making fun of me is out of place on
a snowy morning when we go out in the cold.

Mama stops stuffing biscuits. "Pauline? What are you doing? I've told you before, it's not Christian to mock Arlene."

Water comes to Pauline's eyes. "I am not, Mama. I am not."

"Then why are you wearing that shoe?"

Josh looks up, and Daddy comes in. We wait to hear her answer.

She looks around at us. The kerosene lamp flickers, and the smell of the oatmeal wraps us like a blanket.

"Speak up!" Daddy says.

"Yesterday when Jimmy got hurt he fell. He landed on my foot. It has swelled so, I can't put on my shoe."

"You did ask me first thing if the mill would close on account of the weather. Were you hoping to slack off today?"

"No, Mama. It's not that."

Mama snaps at her. "You said nothing of it last night." Her mouth goes tight. She slaps on the bucket lids. "If you can walk on it, it's probably not broken." She takes a deep breath. "You don't see Arlene complaining because it's cold and there's snow on the ground. Come eat your porridge before it gets cold."

ELEVEN

AFTER MAMA SETS the cook pot to soak in the sink, she blows out the lamp. She hands out the buckets. I take mine.

This morning we do not call out, "Goodbye, Arlene!" *No warm bed for you this morning. No quilt for you to snuggle under. No. You shall see what it's like to work.*

The morning is little lighter than the dark house we leave behind. Only today, white heaps the road and yards like all of the mill cotton escaped during the night, pouring out to settle around the houses. Our breaths fill the air with down.

I do not know how to manage the steps from the stoop. Arlene goes before me. I watch her step down, hop, and then drag her foot. *Step down, hop, and drag. Step down, hop, and drag.* I try it, wishing I had given her the bucket to carry. If only I had a railing to catch. I fear I shall tumble over on my head.

Josh and Daddy move on out of sight, Josh leaping up out of the snow and landing like a big jackrabbit.

"Be careful!" Mama calls. "There is ice underneath."

We reach the road. The hateful shoe pulls at me. It laces up high and swallows my sock. I would jump like Josh, were it not for the shoe and the swollen foot. I would scamper like some furry animal in the dark on its way to its lair, but no. I watch Arlene. *Step ahead, hop, drag, slide.* Mama is right. The snow is one thing, but the frozen sleet waits beneath. *I was here first,* it seems to say. *Remember that. The snow is harmless. I mean business.*

Others join us on the road, one of the boys swooping up a handful to cup into a snowball. He aims it at another. They laugh and call out, but Arlene and I step ahead— *hop, drag, slide*—she is way ahead of me now.

No fair, Arlene. You are used to the shoe. I am not. No fair! If we are racing, she is winning.

Snow has filled my socks, icing my ankles. I have no brown shoes now. When I bring up my legs, I have only white furry feet—one larger and clumsier—that do not wish to work together.

The lights of the mill glow before us, and the sun rises a bit at a time, pale and sickly, as if it has left its deathbed to go to the mill. I see Mama's lunch pail ahead and hear the quiet *swish-swish* as Arlene moves ahead.

Step ahead, hop, drag, and slide. My good foot

goes out beneath me, and I fall in a heap. My ankle cries out. The dinner pail lies just outside my grasp. Every time I start to rise, my foot slips out from under me. *I will not call Arlene. Mama! Mama! Turn back.*

Struggling, I try to rise again, but a pain shoots through my foot. My eyes burn and water. I blink to clear them as I bump again on the ground. My nose drips even though I wipe it on my sweater sleeve. I pound my fists on the snow, my knuckles white. *I shall turn to ice here.*

Swish–swish. Arlene has turned, has come back to me. *Are you laughing at me, sister? Are you laughing now?*

"Can you rise?"

"No," I admit. I don't want her to see my tears. She reaches out a hand.

I take her arm with both hands and pull, but instead of getting up, I pull Arlene down, too. She tumbles beside me, laughing in surprise.

Two birds in the snow, two birds with their wings clipped. No flying today. She turns to me, and I study her face. She has swallowed her laughter and wears only the surprise.

"Try again," she says. "I'll stay sitting down. Push on me."

Raking my good heel back and forth, I search for the soil beneath the ice. Then I push on her shoulder and straighten up. I feel her body give, wavering before I stand. Arlene does as I did, mining for the earth beneath her, taking my arm to get up. I brace, digging in my toes. She pulls herself upright and stoops for the bucket, brushing it off.

"There," I say.

She reaches for my hand. "Follow in my tracks."

Arlene goes in front. I follow her rhythm, stepping exactly where she has walked. The back of her sweater wears a linty coating of frost; her socks and shoes, the same. Her fingers around my hand feel no warmer or colder than my own.

SUCH A CLATTER! I stand at the door of the spinning room, no stranger today. I have a job. As the warmth floods me, my cheeks pulse with the heat. My red hands tingle as they lose their chill, and the snow falls from me in fat drops, leaving my shoes and socks sopping.

Twirling like dancers, the bobbins spin. Some fatten and have to stop for breath, but the lean ones continue their merry jig.

Edwin sits on the floor, his cheeks growing red as he strips down to his bare feet. The whistle sounds, but this time it is a giant owl that perches right above us, howling to be heard above the noise. Even the floor has joined the dance, keeping rhythm with the machines.

Pauline limps in by me, and Mr. Godbold looks first at her and then at me. Pauline points to me. Back again at me. At last he gestures to a corner, where I find a broom and begin to sweep. Glancing back I see Pauline still stands before the dancers as if unsure what she shall do.

"Look sharp, Pauline!" Mr. Godbold calls.

Edwin climbs, stretches, reaches for a stopped twirler, and fastens a thin one in place.

Pauline still hesitates.

Mr. Godbold hollers and points. "There, Pauline, there!"

She tests her foot to step up, but it slips. I keep my broom moving, but I watch as she hangs back, then drops down to take off her own shoe, then Josh's. Her socks plaster her feet, and she plucks the toes to pull them off, but they cling like a second skin, and she must roll them from the top like Mama rolls down her stockings.

So now the mocking one will reveal her true self. We will see now the two flawless feet, the two matched ankles, the ten perfect toes. We will see that she lay in the snow tricking me, making me come back to her as a ruse.

Mr. Godbold yells, pacing the floor toward her. I hold my breath. *The teasing one will get a tongue-lashing for her dalliance.* Her leg jerks as a sock comes off, and her heel strikes the floor. She winces.

So, she was not teasing after all. Her foot is mottled, blue and purple; her toes like fat sausages, plump at the end of her puffed-up foot.

Mr. Godbold looks down, glaring. He shakes his finger before he turns to me again. He gestures to another broom, sending Pauline after it before he kicks aside her discarded clothing and reaches to tie the broken threads himself. His hands are large and awkward, and he fumbles.

Pauline disappears between the tall rows to sweep, and I begin the hunt for lint in earnest. At home, at least, once I find it in its hiding places, I go on to cook or make beds or do wash. Here there is no end to the fluff, like snowflakes. It puddles around bobbins and under the flying thread. Nobody wants it. The spinners dust it off onto the floor, and I must herd it all together in a pile, where it becomes a hill of white furry ants that crawl around in confusion on the trembling floor.

When I scoop up the lint in the pan, some of it takes wing. *Keep still! I am new here, but I understand brooms and lint and flying things. You shall not get the best of me. You shall not get the best of me, for I am like Pauline now.*

I have a job.

TWELVE

I AM OF TWO MINDS. One side of me says, "Now you can see Carrie, Katie, and Margaret, even Mama. Now you can go beyond your row of spinners." The other says, "The shame of it. You can only do what the youngest boys are hired to do—sweep the floor."

Arlene was to have felt the shame, not I.

And my pay. That thought only now occurs to me. I will make a boy's wages for today, the same as Arlene. What a boy makes in a week will not pay the rent or buy the rice at the company store. The money is even less than a doffer brings in. Daddy will frown on Saturday when the pay is given out.

But Jimmy will have no pay. *No pay and no thumb.*

I round the corner where Carrie works. She is slender and lithe, tall enough to reach the broken threads. She doesn't have to climb, but she must scurry to mind her three machines. And what of George in the carding room? They would be together, but all that unites them now is the rumbling floor.

Never before barefooted here, I had not felt the floor except through my shoes. It tugs at my feet, growls at my leg bones, and brings the pulse in my hurt foot. I wonder if my soles grow as black as Jimmy's and Edwin's.

Carrie smiles, showing her even white teeth. Her hair is black, so black it reminds me of a scuttle of coal that might glint blue in the sun. She wears her hair pinned up, away from her oval face; her skin so pale, she might be a glass of milk skimmed of its cream. *Rose Red.* I can see them hand in hand, she and George, slipping off at lunch hour, fleeing to find someone to marry them but held back by the ice. Here, held by the heat.

She looks down at my foot as I draw the broom along. Her smile turns to a frown. Her dark eyes shift to my face. Except for the noise, I know she would ask me, How? How did *that* happen?

Margaret's plaits trail down the back of her print dress. I have seen that dress before. Her older sister wore it until it crept up her knees. Then it was red. Now I think maybe only the inside is that color. It looks the same as some other frocks I have seen, the same pattern cut and sewed from sacks the chicken feed comes in at the store.

Seeing Margaret makes me want to raise my hand to her, but I hate for her to see me doing Edwin's job. But what of that? Because of me, Margaret will not hear Mr. Godbold this morning. No, I have silenced him. He has to work my job, and he cannot yell, "There, Margaret! Look sharp, Margaret!" She is my friend whether she knows it or not. *See what I have done for you?*

Her socks have drooped around her ankles, still wet from the early walk. They will be dry in time for the trip back home.

I could put my shoes and socks back on, I guess, but this way the girls will see I am not Arlene, and Mama will see when I am close to her. She will know I am not Arlene, the lazy one who lolls in bed and claims to be gone from home midwifing babies.

My hands grow tired of the broom. *Horrid thing.* My fingers are small, right for tying threads, not intended to wrap around this handle, this stick of wood that drags with me wherever I go.

Katie, have you brought your jackstones today? What will you play? Eggs in the basket? Crack the eggs? Or shall we begin with ones? Then twos. *I am good at jacks.* But not in the sun today. The snow covers the ground. Ah, we could sit right here on the floor to play, leaving Mr. Godbold to mind the broken threads. A fine joke behind his back.

I will see Mama once before I turn back to find the lint that creeps and hides.

Does Mr. Godbold yell at Mama like he does at Jimmy, Edwin, and me? I cannot believe he does. Mama is quick. She taught me how, long before they paid me to do it, but I must get faster. Katie, Margaret, and I must get swifter, or we shall have only one machine when we are as old as Carrie. Then we will never make any more money than we do today.

Although I stare at Mama's back, she has no eyes for me, only for the strands that wind onto the bobbins.

GUILT NIBBLES AT ME as it did over at Mrs. Harrell's. Today I sweep for pay, but I know at home the chamber pots brim, the oatmeal clings in fat lumps, and the kitchen grows cold.

Who sweeps at the Harrell house today? Who tidies the house, builds up the fire? *"A man can't work on breakfast alone."* Maybe Miss Bertha has gone back to see that dinner is made, that Percy is dry. Mr. Harrell is not like Margaret's daddy. Mr. Harrell has his work at the mill, and he cannot find a cup in his own kitchen. That is someone else's job.

I wonder about Aaron, the new baby, the one who has Percy's place now. Will he feel the wrath of Percy's teeth as he clings to their mother? *Beware the firstborn, the stronger one. Beware. Beware.*

The window beckons to me, but it is off my path. On the sill a small gray spider has set up home, spun a web in the corner. He perches on it, proud. He owns a place there, watching as the bobbins turn, but he has done his reeling out in secret, without any noise. For one moment I start to lift my broom, but I am not paid to sweep away spiders. I have to concentrate on lint.

Snow fills the window, but it is hard to think of anything chilled. In here *cold* is a forgotten word. The heat has arrived, making me think I will never be cold enough again. My hands feel sticky on the broom handle, my shoes and socks drying fast, but my face is damp with sweat. I pause to raise the hair off the back of my neck, looking for a breeze that does not come.

Pauline has disappeared, her trail free of the white stuff; only now that her broom sweeps clear, more falls behind it, brushed down by Mr. Godbold's large, awkward hands.

I think he is angry at Pauline's foot since now he has to do her job. Pauline is no longer perfect. I had to see to believe it. The unflawed one, flawed. Maybe I will mock her now. *Look, Pauline, this is the way you walk. Look at me! See? The little hop-jump I do. I shall teach it to you. I already have!* We could have done it the other way. She could have showed me perfection, but no. *Since you left it up to me, I taught you first.* Or maybe she made fun of me, and it stuck.

That is it!

One night at supper Pauline teased me.

"I'll give you Mr. Godbold's stare." She crossed her eyes and glared at me.

"Stop it, Pauline!" Mama said. She shook her finger. "Stop it this minute, or they'll get stuck. Your eyes will stick like that."

Pauline laughed.

Are you laughing now, hurt bird?

My stomach growls. At home I would be putting on the dinner stew now, readying the tin pails. Today I shall have company to eat dinner with. Where shall we take our meal? Not in the corner in the sun, out of the way of the wind. The corner is piled with snow. Where then? I would like a little bit of the cold to trickle down my back now.

Katie, Margaret, and Pauline. *Will they let me in their games? Will they tell me some of their jokes?*

I listen for the whistle. My ears ring with the noise of the mill, but now I push it from me, so that it roars in another place not so close to my head. That is part of the price I pay to be close to Pauline and the girls, Mama, Daddy, and Josh. I am one of them now. I have a job. I work at the mill.

THIRTEEN

I HAVE SHOWED MY FOOT and proved I cannot climb, even out of my wet socks and shoes. I find them again, dried, where I left them, and put them on. *Josh's shoe has no partner now at home. Both of the old ones have come to work, but Arlene and I each have left one of ours at home. That makes a pair under the bed.*

Grabbing up the bucket, I look for Katie and Margaret, wondering where they'll eat dinner. They will go where we go when it rains, I think, over in the corner of the room where the grown women take their dinner.

Arlene has put her broom away, too, and clumps along beside me to the room, where I shall be glad to sit.

Miss Ethel is already there. She looks up at me and then at Arlene. Surprise causes her to turn and look again at me. She smiles. I will not explain, knowing Mama will tell her about my hurt foot and Arlene.

Margaret's mama comes in, and then Mama. They sit with Miss Ethel at the table. I wait for Katie and Margaret, but after a few minutes, I plop down with the ladies. When the two girls come in, we will move on over with them to have our dinner. At least I will.

Margaret's mother sinks down at the table. "I sent Margaret to watch for Henry. I don't know if they've cleared the road or if the snow has begun to melt." She draws one hand over her face and stifles a yawn.

Mama puts her dinner pail before her. Miss Ethel places hers alongside.

"It took me by surprise," Mama says. "The weather and the new baby—Jimmy's accident." She shakes her head. "Arlene was over at the Harrells', helping Miss Bertha all the afternoon, so the house was at sixes and sevens when we came home. I've done nothing about a pounding for either of them."

Miss Ethel smooths her hair. Close up I can see strands of gray creeping into the red.

"I cut down some of Bobby's things when Percy was born," she says. "Reckon she's still got some of those."

"Arlene," Mama says, "did you take note of the clothes?"

Arlene, Arlene, Arlene.

"Yes, ma'am. She had a stack in the trunk."

"Warm things? Percy was born in the spring."

Arlene hesitates. "There was a blanket we wrapped him in."

"I've a square of flannel," Miss Ethel says. "I could stitch up a sacque out of that."

Still no sign of the girls. Margaret's mama looks over to the door and back to the others. "You all go ahead and eat. Henry will be here after a while. Surely he will."

"We'll wait," Mama says. "It's nothing that's going to get cold. I was thinking this morning I've still got some dried apples left from the fall. I could make a pie for both of them."

"Sugar, Mama," Arlene says.

Mama claps a hand over her own mouth. "That's right. We're out of it."

"I have a little extra," Miss Ethel says.

Margaret's mama drums her fingers on the table. "I do wish you'd go ahead and eat your dinner."

The "tin-bucket toter" is late. My stomach growls. And Katie? Her younger brother must be tardy as well. I finger the lid of my pail, but I know to open it would be rude. Mama would not excuse it. So we wait until Katie and Margaret finally come in.

Margaret leans down to speak to her mother in low tones, but I hear her nevertheless. "Daddy hasn't come. I went down to the front and looked down the road. No sign of him."

Margaret's mama reaches out to pat her hand. "It's all right. It won't kill us to wait to eat 'til tonight."

Katie hangs back, but I see she has no pail, either. "Come on, Margaret. Let's play. I brought my jacks."

Mama opens her dinner, takes out her ham biscuit, and breaks it. She puts one of the halves before Margaret's mama.

"No," the other woman protests. "I couldn't."

"Of course you can," says Mama. "Don't be silly. You'd do the same for me, wouldn't you?"

"Yes, but somehow it doesn't seem right."

Katie and Margaret go off to the side. I see their heads bowed over their game. Katie has started bouncing the ball. I want to play with them. I am hungry, but I want to play with them more than I want to eat. I hear them laughing as Margaret scampers to fetch the runaway ball.

I watched as Mama made up the dinner buckets this morning. I know that Josh and Daddy each have two biscuits, that Mama has one, and that Arlene and I have one biscuit apiece in the same pail. *Where is the rice that shines like pearls in the sun? Where are the chunks of cabbage, the little morsels of meat? I will give my* biscuit to them, and they will invite me to play.

Lifting the lid I take out one of the biscuits and shove the pail to Arlene. "Here." I feel her watching me as I cross the room.

Katie looks up at me as I limp. "Hello."

I hold out the biscuit. "Why don't you divide this?"

They both smile at me. *Next they will make room for me; ask me to sit down with them.*

Katie says, "Thank you, Arlene."

I am not Arlene. "Pauline," I say, correcting her. I stand waiting as they tear the bread and ham apart, and each one puts a half to her mouth. The biscuit disappears. Their jaws work in unison as they go back to their game.

"Where were we, Katie?" Margaret asks, cramming the last of the crumbs into her mouth.

"Twos. You have to go back and start

again at twos. You dropped the ball. You fouled."

"That's right," says Margaret. "So I did."

They turn their backs to me as Margaret scatters the jackstones on the floor.

My foot hurts as I head back to the table. Arlene has been watching me. *What are you looking at, sister?*

I am a fool. I gave my dinner away so the girls would make me their friend.

Arlene says nothing. She takes her biscuit with the golden top. The ham, pink and fat, peeks out around the edge. My mouth waters, but I turn away. *I shall not watch you eat it. You know I am a fool.*

She has nothing to gain. But she scores the biscuit in two and hands me one half.

EVERY DAY WHEN I had delivered the dinner, I came back to the empty house to eat my own noon meal. It was still warm but held no surprises. I'd think of the others unsnapping the lids. *"Oh! What have we here? Stew with bits of white potatoes and orange cuts of carrots, buttered corn bread on the top."* Or *"What has she fixed today? Why, Arlene has stewed up a chicken with dumplings on the side."*

But I always knew what was waiting at home on the stove, since I'd smelled it and tasted it for seasoning half the morning. *No. No surprises.*

The house would ring with quiet, only my

spoon clinking on the tin pan. I could almost hear Josh with the men, bragging of fish caught in the river or laughing about old Roscoe Jenkins rip-roaring drunk on Saturday night and sentenced to church for six Sundays in a row. They'd be guffawing at the mill while I ate at home to the tune of a chiming spoon.

Josh and Daddy with the other men, Mama with the ladies, and Pauline with her two friends.

But today when the whistle blows, I am here with them.

I put my broom away and follow Pauline, who carries the dinner pail and leads to the room, where I see Miss Ethel already sits.

She looks up at Pauline and then at me. Surprise causes her to turn and look again at Pauline. She smiles. I will not explain, knowing Mama will tell her about Pauline's hurt foot and why I am working today.

Margaret's mama comes in, and then Mama. They sit with Miss Ethel at the table. I guess Pauline waits for Katie and Margaret, but after a few minutes, she plops down with the ladies. When the two girls come in, I suppose we will move on over with them to have our dinner.

Margaret's mother sinks into a chair. "I sent Margaret to watch for Henry. I don't know if they've cleared the road or if the snow has begun to melt." She draws one hand over her face and stifles a yawn.

Mama sets her dinner pail down. Miss Ethel sets hers right beside it.

"It took me by surprise," Mama says, and then I stop listening and watch Pauline watch for the other girls.

"Arlene," Mama says, bringing me back, "did you take note of the clothes?"

Soft. With the faded rose. "Yes, ma'am. She had a stack in the trunk."

"Warm things? Percy was born in the spring."

I didn't pay close attention. I hesitate. "There was a blanket we wrapped him in."

"I've a square of flannel," Miss Ethel says. "I could stitch up a sacque out of that."

Still no sign of the girls. Margaret's mama says, "You all go ahead and eat. Henry will be here after a while. Surely he will."

"We'll wait," Mama says. "It's nothing that's going to get cold. I was thinking this morning I've still got some dried apples left from the fall. I could make a pie for both of them."

I couldn't make the cake. We have no sugar. "Sugar, Mama," I say.

"That's right. We're out of it."

"I have a little extra," Miss Ethel says.

Margaret's mama sighs. "I do wish you'd go ahead and eat your dinner."

My stomach growls. Pauline fingers the lid of the pail but does not open it. We wait. Finally Katie and Margaret come in.

Margaret whispers to her mother, but I hear her. "Daddy hasn't come. I went down to the front and looked down the road. No sign of him."

Margaret's mama touches her hand. "It's all right. It won't kill us to wait to eat 'til tonight."

"Come on, Margaret," Katie says. "Let's play. I brought my jacks." She has no pail, either.

Mama opens her pail and breaks her ham biscuit. She puts one half in front of Margaret's mama.

"No. I couldn't."

"Of course you can," says Mama. "Don't be silly. You'd do the same for me, wouldn't you?"

"Yes, but somehow it doesn't seem right."

Katie and Margaret go off. Pauline will be joining them soon. I want to play with them, with the three of them. I hear them laughing.

Prying up the lid of our pail, Pauline takes out one of the biscuits and shoves the pail toward me. "Here." But she doesn't eat. She rises, the plump bread in hand, and goes to the girls.

Should I follow?

But she doesn't sit down with them. Instead, she holds the food out. Smiling, they take it. She continues to stand, watching as they stuff it into their mouths before turning their backs to her. Margaret scatters the jackstones on the floor.

Pauline turns to come back to the table. She looks disappointed. She's given her dinner away and has nothing to show for it.

Katie and Margaret have each other. *Don't you understand, Pauline? Things come in twos. Mama and Daddy, Carrie and George, Margaret and Katie. The two of Josh's old shoes. The good shoes we wear. The other two shoes left under the bed. They all come in twos, even you and I. Only when there is just one is there any room for a two.*

I say nothing, but taking my sandwich out of the pail, I score it in two and give one half to her.

FOURTEEN

Saturday! *Saturday!*

Today the joke is on the whistle. Oh, the old crone calls all right. She shrieks the same, and we go to her as if we must obey her to the letter, but today is Saturday, and we will stay only until noon. She may screech all she likes, but come dinnertime, we will escape her. *You may think we are just going to eat, that we will come back. Oh no. No matter how loud you cry at one o'clock, you cannot coax us back.*

I put on one sock and turn my attention to the other foot. Its purple streaks have turned a sickly yellow, and it no longer throbs in the night. The swelling is less, but I still reach for Josh's shoe, which has comforted me this week.

Arlene thumps around the bed as she spreads up the covers. I answer her thump with my shoe and plump up the pillows. We laugh.

Today we carry no dinner pails. They will rest in the stove room until the start of the week. Mama will cook us a proper dinner today and tomorrow, too, after church. After four days of just bread and cold meat, my stomach yearns for hot stew. Daddy might catch a fish or two at the river this afternoon, dredge it in cornmeal, and fry it up crisp in hot lard. There is always bread with the fish, to keep the bones from getting stuck in your throat.

I go out first thing, and the early light barely shows the leftover snow. It is like scant icing on gingerbread cake. I step in a patch on the way to pee, and the ice clings to my ankle.

Saturday morning is better than afternoon because we still have the rest of the day, and Daddy smiles as he comes in from the privy to wash up. Every minute that ticks away after that brings us closer to Monday morning.

He rubs his hands together. "Snow still hanging around."

Mama turns from the stove. "It's waiting for more. That's what the old-timers say. When the snow stays on the ground, more will fall soon."

"Mr. Godbold thinks Jimmy will be back on Monday," Daddy says.

"So soon?" Mama frowns. "When I went over there, he complained of the pain. Said his thumb hurts him." Mama ladles out grits.

Arlene passes a bowl to me. I hand it to Daddy.

Why would his thumb pain him now? He has not one to hurt unless he speaks of the one he has left.

Daddy picks up his spoon. He glances down at his other hand. He closes his three fingers over the nubs. "That it will for a good long time. It is worse in the cold." He blows on a spoonful of grits before he brings it up to his lips. "He will get used to it. He is young, after all."

If Jimmy goes back to work, and my foot is well, all will be as before. We will have hot dinner in the buckets at noon and clean clothes when we come home. Arlene will see to that.

I call for my hate. It does not answer me. I should like it close by if I need it, but this morning it has left me alone, and I cannot remember where it is.

MORE OF THE SNOW has melted today, a slow oozing, but at noontime the sun has gone in, and a stinging wind whips at us on the way home. It makes me want to hide my hands in my sweater sleeves and pull the wool closer to my neck. I look at Pauline. Her nose is red; her cheeks, chapped. I know I look the same.

Carrie and George pass. She gives him a sidelong glance and a smile.

Mama has gone ahead, picking her way along the muddy road, careful of puddles, her skirt held up in one hand. Today is payday. She will stop at the store for sugar.

I smell woodsmoke. The houses along the way puff from their stove-room chimneys, tall pipes, but the wind steals the smoke like it does our sweat from the spinning room.

Mama has hurried, and when we get home she has pork chops frying and water boiling. "When the wash is done, we'll eat dinner," she says.

Except for this week, I would already have the clothes on the line. I begin at the sink, steam rising, and stoop for the clothes. Pauline is at my elbow. *Move, sister, you are in my way. We'll never get to pork chops and gravy if you insist on getting underfoot.* But when I turn back she has taken up the scrub board and reaches out for the overalls I have in my hand.

We clunk down the steps into the yard, the basket between us. The cold is less now because the stove room grows warm, and we will be out only as long as it takes to hang the clothes.

Josh is splitting wood by the time we duck back into the house. The ax rings. The wood thuds. Splinters fly. *Precious ones.* I shall come back later to gather the little pieces. He has no patience for piling them together. Only the whack of the ax speaks to him.

When we sit down, Mama sets out dinner on the table. Boiled potatoes covered in brown gravy and the chops seared brown with a ring of fat. She places a plate of biscuits before Daddy.

Josh lifts his fork. Mama gives him a half teasing frown and shakes her head. He puts down his silverware and waits for Daddy to bow his head.

"Thank you, Lord, for dinner," Daddy says. "Amen."

The potatoes burn the roof of my mouth,

and I try to make myself wait for the next mouthful. Josh sops his bread in the gravy and makes chewing noises. Mama flashes him a look I know he would understand if he were paying attention to anything except his plate.

Mama says, "This afternoon I'll make two sponge cakes. One for the Harrells." She smiles. "I don't think anybody's baked there this week." She turns to me. "And when you have milked the Widow Wade's cow, we'll give them some of ours. Frances's milk should be coming in. She needs extra to drink herself."

Because it's Saturday and cold, Mama makes Daddy a cup of coffee after his meal. He pours some into his saucer to cool and takes out his pipe. He slurps, then fills his pipe from the pouch in his pocket. He reaches over for a match, and drawing it across the bottom of his shoe, he strikes it flaring. The sharp smell of the match and the tobacco take over the meat and coffee.

We wait. Only Mama rises to carry the stack of dirty dishes to the sink.

It is settlement time. Usually I turn away from this, knowing I have no reason to stay at the table on payday after dinner is done, but today there might be something that belongs to me in Daddy's pocket.

He looks around at us. "What are you all expecting?" A grin creeps onto his face.

"Come on, Daddy," Josh says. "It's pay-day."

"Is that a fact?"

Even Josh laughs. "Yes, that's a fact."

Daddy raises his hand like he would run his fingers through his hair, but instead he reaches to the top pocket of his overalls and withdraws the brown envelope, laying it on the table.

More suspense. *Daddy, come on.*

"Mama, do you know why these children sit here, what they're waiting for?"

"No, sirree. I haven't a notion." Mama smiles.

"Josh, you're going to play kickball this afternoon with the boys?" Daddy asks.

"I thought about it. Yes, sir," Josh says.

"Well, I guess I better get my business over with so you can be on your way."

We all take a deep breath. Daddy pulls back the flaps to expose some bills and change. He counts it out, his finger stubs touching the coins as he slides them into piles. "We've got some extra this payday. Josh, here's your share after the rent." He pushes four quarters to Josh, who scoops them up. "Pauline, here's yours." He counts out two dimes, two pennies, and a nickel. Then he turns to me. "Arlene, you've paid your rent this month, too. Here's fifteen cents for you."

Fifteen cents! That's peppermints or chewing gum or johnnycakes from the barrel at the company store. I am rich! This one day, I am rich.

FIFTEEN

A FEW BROWN CRUMBS still cling to the baking pan. I slide my finger along the edge. Arlene watches me and does the same at the other end of the pan. *Monkey see, monkey do.*

"Get the other pan," I say. "This is mine." I pop my finger into my mouth as Arlene turns to the second one.

Mama has filled the sink with soapy water, and she is reaching for the pan. Arlene squeals, "No, Mama, not yet. Give me the crumbs before you wash it."

I tighten my grip on the warm tin.

Mama laughs. "You two! Don't get lost

between here and the Harrells'. If you do, I'll know what happened to my cakes."

After wrapping them in clean cloths, Mama hands each of us a cake. Mine is still warm and soft, smelling of vanilla. The crumbs melt in my mouth. I look at Arlene and grin, and she grins back, her hands filled with cake, too.

Out front I turn to Arlene. "Where will you go—to Jimmy's?"

She frowns. "I should like to see little Aaron again."

I have never seen a baby so young. "Me, too, but I should also like to see Jimmy."

"Yes," Arlene says. "I would, too, but I have to milk before dark. Widow Wade's cow doesn't know it's Saturday, and I want to go to the store." Her voice trails off.

I am curious about the milking she does, since we don't have a cow. "Is there time for it all if I help with the cow?"

She stifles a giggle, then sobers. "What do you know of cows?"

"Not much," I admit, "but I could help carry the can home."

"Yes, it has two handles."

We both of us look like fools standing out in the road. "Then let's go," I say.

Mr. Harrell opens the door and stands there in his undershirt. "Come in," he barks. He smells of perspiration and beer.

We limp to the stove room, where Mrs. Harrell sits, the baby at her breast. Percy leans against the chair at her side.

Arlene puts the cake on the table. "Mama sent this, Mrs. Harrell."

Mrs. Harrell looks at us both, even down to our shoes. She stumbles over her words. "I've never seen you two together before. Why, which is which?"

"I'm Arlene. I was with you when Aaron was born."

"Oh yes." Mrs. Harrell smiles. "So you were. And you left my house as clean as a whistle, and I am most obliged. For that and the washing and all."

"You're welcome," Arlene says.

"How does Percy like his new brother?" I ask.

"He's not sure yet," she says. "I think he wishes he was the only one still, but they'll have each other when no one else is around."

Arlene looks at the clock. "We have other places to go."

We find Jimmy out in back of his house.

"Pauline?" He looks puzzled. "Who is who?"

I step forward.

One of his hands is wrapped in white. The other grips an ax. His eyes light up at the sight of the cake. "I'm trying to learn the other hand. I ain't good at it yet." He shrugs.

"I used to chop wood with two. One hand ain't much good—not yet. They tell me I hurt your foot."

I remember the old shoe and look down. "It's all right. It's better now."

As we head to the store, a thought occurs to me: I have twenty-seven cents. I could get the jackstones, put the rest on the books for next payday. I have heard of others doing that. *Yes. I shall have my jacks. Today I shall have them.* My money clinks in my pocket. *I shall have them.*

My NICKEL AND DIME jangle in my pocket. *Which shall it be? Peppermints or horehound drops? Johnnycakes or butterscotch?* We must hurry. I should have my mind made up before I get there. Saturday afternoon on payday is no time to stand around not knowing what to buy. I have not had peppermints since Christmas, and when I think of that morning, I remember them at the foot of the bed beside an orange. I held the orange to me, inhaling the skin of it, not wanting to eat it because then it would be gone. But the peppermints, sharp and biting sweet. *Better than butterscotch that bathes the tongue? I cannot say, but johnnycakes are gone faster, swallowed and gone. Peppermints and horehounds stay. Which?*

The store is crowded. Old Roscoe Jenkins sits playing checkers by the stove, a jar of pickled pigs' feet beside him. The store smells of sawdust, stale beer, and sauerkraut.

Through the crowd I glimpse the counters of glass jars; the candies, jewels gleaming. *Which?*

Margaret waves to us, coming over, elbowing her way through the crowd. She looks at us for a moment as if she might ask, Which? but she breaks into chatter. "Did you know George and Carrie ran away this afternoon? Did you know they got married?"

I am not surprised.

She pushes a braid back on her shoulder. "We'll serenade them tonight. After supper."

Pauline looks at her. "A serenade?"

"Yes. You know—with tin cans. I'm collecting them. See if you have any at home. Bye."

What will Pauline buy? She hasn't said.

She pushes her way to the counter. I still haven't decided. I follow her. At the glass case she stops and looks down. Eight silver jackstones circle a bright red ball. To the side, a blue leather pouch with a drawstring.

Pauline turns to me. "See?" She hurries her next words. "But you come here all the time to buy things for the house." She takes out her twenty-seven cents. "You must show me how to charge part of the cost for next payday."

"You mean put it on the books?"

She nods. "I can pay it off next time Daddy has extra."

Daddy's words sing in my head. *Food to feed hungry young'uns or kerosene to light a dark house. No foolishness goes on the books.*

"Jacks are 'foolishness.'"

Pauline's eyes narrow. "Not if I want them."

So are hard candies. "I'm telling you what Daddy says." *You must start with a one to have a two.* "Could I play with them?"

"Of course. The two of us could play. Tonight after supper, after the Widow Wade's cow. After the serenade. We could play eggs in the basket or crack the eggs. You wouldn't tell Daddy?"

"Of course not. But he would find out. He would know if you charged on the books."

"Then I shan't have them."

"How much are they?"

"Forty cents." She hangs her head. "I have only twenty-seven."

Peppermints fade. I reach in my pocket for the change. I put it besides hers. "No, *we* shall have them, paid in full."

She smiles. I know from the corners of my own mouth and the sight of her face as I smile back at her, we are alike. We are twins.

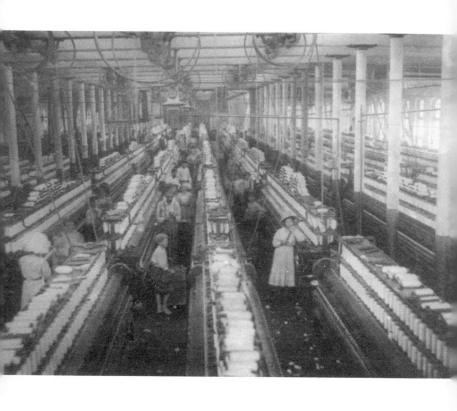

AFTERWORD

In 1905 many children like Pauline, Arlene, Jimmy, Edwin, Katie, and Margaret worked. They held jobs on farms and in factories, mills, and coal mines. They delivered newspapers and telegrams, or shined shoes on the street instead of going to school.

Their hours were long; their pay, small. Oftentimes the jobs they did were lonely, boring, tiring, and dangerous.

In the first few decades of the twentieth century, many people began to take a different look at children working and started to question whether it was a fair thing to keep children away from schooling to do adult jobs.

One such person was the photographer Lewis W. Hine, who traveled the United States from 1908 to 1912, taking pictures of youngsters in their workplaces. Seeing his photos, many more people were convinced that young children had no place in the labor market, and eventually child labor was abolished in the United States.

READER CHAT PAGE

1. Would you rather take on the daily duties of Pauline or Arlene? Whose life do you think is more difficult, and why?

2. Life is very hard for the twins and the rest of their family. What are some of the small pleasures that make their days more bearable?

3. One day a stranger comes into the factory and takes photographs of Pauline and some of the other child laborers. What is his purpose? How do the twins' parents feel about his presence?

4. Miss Bertha tells Arlene that when she and Pauline were born, their father hung his head and said, "Mother, we are undone! We are ruined!" What do you think he meant by that comment?

5. Why is Mrs. Harrell's husband disappointed when their new baby is a boy? What are the advantages of being female in this mill town? What are the disadvantages?

6. What are the circumstances that allow Pauline and Arlene to finally understand each other?